AF270128

Given

Isabelle Taylor

Publisher's Note: This is a work of fiction. Names, characters, places, and incidents are a product of the author's imagination. Locales and public names are sometimes used for atmospheric purposes. Any resemblance to actual people, living or dead, or to businesses, companies, events, institutions, or locales is completely coincidental.

KDP Paperback ISBN: 978-1-991416-02-5

IngramSpark Paperback ISBN: 978-1-991416-00-1

IngramSpark Hardcover ISBN: 978-1-991416-01-8

Content Warnings

Bondage (and penetration) with sentient vines, painful sex, pain kink, size kink, inhuman genitalia, poison, crying during sex, aphrodisiac sex pollen, sex under the influence (of sex pollen), violence.

And like all of my books, the MCs are childfree by choice.

One

Vale was being Summoned.

He paused, one claw poised to trim a shadowy vine. Who was summoning him? Was one of his Skull-stalker brothers in trouble?

Vale bowed his antlered head, concentrating. It did not feel like a fellow Skullstalker. It felt like a mortal, pulling him weakly toward the mortal realm.

Vale dropped the vine, considering. He did not *have* to obey the Summoning. The spell was weak. If he put the slightest amount of pressure on it, it would snap as easily as a rib-twig branch.

But Vale was curious. He had not been Summoned in an age. And never by a mortal. It was likely a useless affair, but he could spare a moment to see to it.

Well, he considered, staring around the twisted, messy overgrowth that made up the wilderness void nowadays. *I cannot reasonably spare a moment. But I am surely due for a rest.*

The idea made him uncomfortable. He had not rested in years. There was too much work to do. Once, he'd had magical assistants to help him tend to the plants, keeping them healthy and content. But the assistants died centuries before. Perhaps millennia. It was difficult to keep track these days.

Vale strode through the thick black bushes to the silver pool that allowed him to travel between realms. But before he could step into it, something surprising happened: a bone tulip stretched out its chalky petals and curled around his wrist.

Vale looked down at it, shocked. Once, the void communed with him often. Nowadays, when a leaf brushed the skull mask that made up most of his face, it was simply the wind.

He touched the bone tulip reassuringly.

"I will be back soon," he assured it.

The bone tulip shivered against his cool skin. The void was trying to say something. But try as it might, no words or even a fleeting emotion appeared in Vale's head.

Vale unwound the bone tulip gently from his wrist. Then he closed his glowing green eyes and stepped into the silver pool, letting the Summoning drag him away.

The mortal realm stunk of blood.

Vale's fanged mouth watered. He opened his eyes to see a dark forest. It was plain, sparse, and silent. Not like his own void, where crowded shadows dripped and faraway beasts cawed.

There was a circle drawn around him in the dirt, the exact shape of the pool he had just stepped into. It was crafted with the same blood that smelled so enticing upon his arrival.

The source of the blood was obvious: directly in front of him lay a plump young woman tied to a decrepit stone slab. Her wrists and ankles were bound with silk, her right arm dripping blood onto her white dress. The blood was almost as bright as her hair, which was wrapped in a crimson braid around her head.

This woman was the source of the Summoning, Vale realized. The weak tug of magic ended with her.

An older mage stood next to her, sweating hard, a staff clutched in his hands. The one who cast the spell, Vale decided. His attire was luxurious but tattered. He had the same features as the woman, plump and crimson-haired. Unlike the woman, he looked positively delighted to see the Skullstalker appear.

Further into the forest, a group of humans gasped at Vale. Several of them gripped arrows or held up axes.

"Be still," the mage barked. He wiped his damp forehead and gave Vale a triumphant grin.

Vale had never been smiled at by a mortal before. His brief encounters with mortals usually included screaming, running, and occasionally a meal. They were decent food, if Vale could be bothered to make the journey to the mortal realm.

"What did I tell you?" the mage declared, lifting his staff.

There was a vial tied onto the end that dangled annoyingly every time it moved.

"He appears, just as I proclaimed!" the mage continued. "Another victory for the Circle of the Jeweled Fist."

A reverent murmur echoed around the group huddled behind them. Vale paid them no mind. He was transfixed by the mysterious woman on the stone slab.

She was terrified. He could smell it on her sweat-slick skin. But for some reason, it hardly showed on her face. If he couldn't smell the fear rolling off of her in waves, he would think she was merely nervous.

"Mighty Skullstalker," the mage declared. "I am Christopher Silverpetal! I present my dutiful niece, whom I prize above all things, as a sacrifice."

The woman's face went pale. She looked over at her uncle in alarm. "Trade! You said trade!"

"A trade, of course." Christopher bowed his head to Vale. "My apologies, Skullstalker. My tongue slipped. My point is, she is yours. Take her back to your wilderness void and do whatever you wish with her. In exchange, you will give my circle a boon."

"A boon," Vale repeated suspiciously.

"Yes!" Christopher straightened his shabby robes eagerly. Even that small movement made the vial dangling from his staff swing irritatingly, and Vale had to resist the urge to snap it off so it would stop distracting him.

"Your wilderness void hosts many strange and powerful plants," Christopher continued. "We would have whatever is best to defeat our enemies. Poisons that have no antidote in our realm. Wood that cannot be burned by mortal fire. Pollen that explodes in burning toxins! Do you have these?"

"I have many dangerous plants," Vale admitted. "But none of them have been tested on mortals."

"That's fine!" Christopher grinned harder. Another drop of sweat ran down his face, plastering his red hair to his forehead. "Whatever you grant us, we will be eternally grateful."

Vale growled, considering. He had never entered into a deal with mortals in the past. But he could spare some plants—more than a few, as his void was so overgrown. Whoever the mortals wished to kill with those plants was none of his business.

But the woman...

He *could* eat her. He was overdue for a meal. He last ate weeks ago, or possibly months.

Or, Vale thought, remembering his light-mote assistants who had died so long ago. *I could take her as an assistant.* If he had someone else to help—even a mortal, who was so much smaller and less capable—he could even get his void under control. Make it balanced and content again, the way it used to be.

Vale loomed over the stone slab. The young woman flinched, pulling her limbs in like she wanted to curl into a ball, only to be stopped by the ropes. Her face betrayed only a hint of the primal fear he could smell on her. It was overpowering, even thicker than the blood dripping from her arm.

She must have volunteered, Vale decided. Otherwise, she would be screaming and struggling for her freedom. A brave thing to do, with her uncle insisting he could do whatever he wished to her once he brought her back to his void.

Vale straightened. The group of humans—the Circle, as Christopher had called them—gripped their weapons warily, watching Christopher for an order.

"I will need time," Vale told Christopher. "To gather your boon."

"That's fine!" Christopher said again, his face ruddy with leftover perspiration from channeling the Summoning spell. "Actually, we have a date. One month from now."

"One month," Vale repeated. He looked at the evening sky, considering. Time ran out of step with the mortal realm in many Skullstalker voids, but his void was not one of them. "That is acceptable."

Christopher nodded, the vial tied to his staff swinging wildly with the motion. "Fantastic! So, do you accept our trade?"

He gestured at his niece, who stared up at Vale nervously.

Something foreign stirred in Vale's chest. Her eyes were huge and full of tears, which she was trying desperately to blink back. Vale was struck by their intense green, so much brighter than her uncle's. If they got any brighter, they could even rival his own.

"Mighty Skullstalker?" Christopher prompted.

Vale tore his gaze away from the woman's fearful face. "I accept."

Christopher sagged in relief. "That's wonderful. Isn't that wonderful, everyone?"

He turned to his Circle behind him. The group made noises of agreement, though none of them let go of their weapons.

Christopher gave them a brash grin. Then he jogged up to Vale, motioning for him to lean down. It was such an absurd request that Vale considered eating him for it. Then he leaned down obediently, curious what this sweaty mage would say and still tempted to snatch that annoying vial swinging from his staff.

Christopher spoke softly. "Do yourself a favor, don't eat her first thing. I am assured my niece has *many* skills. You will find her very useful."

There was something pointed under his words. Vale could not figure out what. He straightened and turned toward the woman, one sharp claw outstretched.

She flinched again, then forced herself to stay still. Vale watched her with detached interest as he sliced through her bindings. He could not help but wonder what she was thinking. He had not told them what he was planning, after all. For all she knew, he planned to devour her the moment he took her back to his void, as her uncle assumed.

The last silk rope snapped. Vale lifted the woman into his arms, surprised by how light she was. He had never held a human before. This one was satisfyingly plump, more so than any mortal of Christopher's Circle. But she fit easily in his arms, barely heavier than a spinetree branch.

Vale resumed his spot in the middle of the bloody Summoning circle the mortals had drawn into the dirt.

"Until next time, dearest niece," Christopher called, waving his staff at her.

The woman lifted a timid hand, red with her own blood.

"Farewell," she called cautiously.

Vale closed his eyes and thought of his void.

The dirt opened up and swallowed him, and the woman in his arms gasped and clung to him. Before he could assure her that all was well, they were rising again—this time out of the silver pool he had stepped into minutes before.

The comforting scent of his void washed over him, all sulphur and ash. He had been amongst it for so long, he had forgotten what it was like without it.

"We are here," he announced, depositing the human woman onto the mossy ground.

She stood, wobbling. For a moment, she merely gaped at their surroundings: leaves dripping darkness, boneplants glowing silver, dark birds flying overhead, the silver pool they had stepped out of. Everything thrummed with an invisible pulse that could only be described as a heartbeat.

However, *she* could not sense the thrum. She was only mortal, after all. But there was a moment where she stared behind them into the silver pool they had entered through, and she looked almost... enchanted. Like this void was not to be feared, but to be cherished.

Then that moment ended.

The woman whirled to him, her terror thick in the air. "D-don't eat me yet, okay?"

Vale wondered who the Circle of the Jeweled Fist was trying to kill. They must be important if they were willing to risk her.

"I have many skills," the woman blurted, brushing her crimson hair out of her face and only succeeding in smearing her bloody arm across her cheek. She winced, wiping it off her face. "I'm a hard worker! I can set traps, and make clothes, and read—"

Vale cut her off. "I did not bring you here to eat you."

"Oh!" The woman did not look relieved, though she was still trying to hide her fear. She actually smiled this time, small and tremulous. "What did you bring me here for?"

Her uncle's words echoed through Vale's head: *she has many skills.* Why did he think her uncle was not talking about her ability to read?

The woman stared up at him, those green eyes so alluring that Vale almost found himself leaning in.

Almost.

"To tend the void," Vale said instead. "I need an assistant."

Two

Ivy's breath left her in a relieved whoosh.

Her uncle had urged her to seduce the beast. *Seduce* him! All because of the stories of the Bygone Queen, where a human witch entranced a Skullstalker into making her his queen.

As if Ivy was capable of seducing *anyone*, let alone a Skullstalker. Until she had seen the Skullstalker in person, she didn't even know it had *lips*. She always heard their whole face was a skull, not just the top part.

"Unless you would prefer me to eat you," the Skullstalker continued in that deep, gravelly voice that sounded like a warning even when he wasn't growling.

Ivy startled. She had been silent far too long, she realized in a panic.

"No!" she said with a nervous laugh. "This is good! I'll be a perfect servant, I swear."

"Assistant," the Skullstalker corrected.

"Assistant," Ivy said faintly. "Yes."

Was *assistant* better than *servant*? It had to be. Her uncle had an assistant when he worked at the palace. He was treated well enough. Also, unlike assistants, servants didn't get to quit. Was this Skullstalker being... *kind* to her? She doubted it.

Skullstalkers were the worst thing a mortal could encounter. They weren't mindless, bloodthirsty beasts. No, they were bloodthirsty beasts who were at *least* as intelligent as a human. Ivy had been hoping to appeal to that intelligent side to buy her enough time to do what she was sent here to do.

Her injured arm throbbed. Ivy hissed in pain, lifting her arm to examine the cut. It had dripped blood all over her white linen dress, which was strangely dry despite emerging through that silver pool.

"You are distracted by your wound," said the Skullstalker.

"No," Ivy tried, wiping her bloody arm with her stained dress. "I'm focused. I can work!"

The Skullstalker ignored her, striding through the strange, thick foliage.

Ivy hesitated. This was no ordinary forest. Every plant was unfamiliar, dripping shadow or dust or shining from the inside out. There were trees made of bones and, alarmingly, a decaying frog climbing placidly up a pulsing tree. Everywhere she looked boasted new, unnatural features.

Part of her was fascinated. But it would be more fascinating if she were simply reading about this place instead of being dropped in the middle of it. This place was not used to mortals. What if it hurt her?

The Skullstalker stopped, turning back to look at her expectantly. "Come."

Then he vanished through the dark trees.

Ivy clenched the vial in her pocket and looked back at the silver pool behind them. She would remember its location and find her way back. She *had* to.

Ivy hurried through the trees after the Skullstalker. Shadowy leaves brushed her skin, but they did not sting or burn like she had been expecting. They simply brushed past like regular leaves. When the dripping shadows touched her, they dissolved on contact.

Maybe her uncle had taken pity on her and suggested the assistant idea, she pondered as she followed the Skullstalker through the bush. Maybe that was what he'd whispered to the Skullstalker at the end. The idea warmed her heart. Her uncle was not a sentimental man, but he *did* care about her. Even if he had been awfully distant since he'd been banished from the royal circle and had to make his own.

Ivy was so busy admiring her horrifying surroundings that she didn't notice the Skullstalker had stopped until she ran into him.

"*Oof*," she said, grabbing the Skullstalker's robes on instinct. She let go immediately, mortified. "Sorry! I didn't mean to. I won't do it again."

The Skullstalker peered down at her curiously. Ivy smiled as wide as she could, trying to look like she was too useful to eat.

"You apologize a lot," the Skullstalker said finally.

"Sorry," Ivy whispered, then winced. "I mean—shit. I'll stop."

The Skullstalker cocked his head at her again. He had moss on his skull, Ivy noticed. Dark green moss climbed his cheekbones and even parts of his antlers. But his robes were untouched, no moss or dirt or even leaves spotting the dark material, which looked like it was carved from nighttime itself.

Ivy almost wanted to touch it. But the Skullstalker's fangs stopped her, not to mention his long claws and threatening height. He could rip her to pieces in a second if he wanted to.

But if he *did* want to, he was restraining himself. Which was... nice? Certainly a relief. For Ivy *and* the Circle, who were counting on her to do something very important as soon as the Skullstalker turned his back.

The Skullstalker reached up. Ivy flinched again, unable to stop it. But the Skullstalker only picked a glowing leaf hanging above her head and slid it into his mouth, chewing neatly.

He took her injured arm and leaned over it, opening his jaw. His tongue lolled out. Ivy stared, her cheeks heating. His tongue was so *long*. Long and pink and oddly alluring in a way she had never considered before.

A thin stream of glowing leaf-spit dripped from the tip of his tongue. Ivy tensed, but the green spit washed over her cut with a pleasant numbing sensation.

The Skullstalker rubbed the leaf-spit into her wound,

spreading the tingling numbness. His fingers were cool and smooth, his claws retracting. Ivy's skin prickled in a way that had nothing to do with the healing herb he was rubbing into her. She couldn't remember the last time she was touched so gently. *This* was the dreaded ruler of the wilderness void?

"What is that?" Ivy asked.

"Soothepine," the Skullstalker explained.

He lifted her arm, examining the cut. The bleeding had stopped. So had the glow from the soothepine.

"Thank you," Ivy whispered.

The Skullstalker looked up, as if remembering that her arm was attached to something. He dropped it, standing back.

"As I told your uncle," he said, "none of these plants have been used on your kind."

"We will gladly take whatever you can spare," Ivy replied. She touched her arm wondrously, mesmerized by the healing cut. It looked like it had been healing for weeks, not minutes.

The Skullstalker took off again. Ivy stumbled after him, looking behind her and trying to remember the path back to the silver pool. They hadn't been walking far; surely she could find it again.

"I'm so grateful to you for keeping me as an assistant," she called as she followed the Skullstalker through the thick leaves. "I love plants. Truly! I am even named after one. Ivy."

"Ivy," the Skullstalker repeated. His guttural voice made her shiver. It took her a moment to recognize his tone: he didn't sound familiar with the plant.

"Do you not have ivy in your void?" Ivy asked cautiously.

"No," the Skullstalker said.

Ivy thought that would be the end of it. But after several seconds of following him, the Skullstalker asked, "What is it?"

"It's a vine," Ivy said hastily. "It's..."

A clinging, strangling, invasive species that people want to get rid of, whispered a voice in her head that sounded alarmingly like the bullies who tormented her back when she lived in a castle with her uncle. The memories were hazy; she left the castle so young, stumbling after her uncle as he swore vengeance to the royals who unfairly banished him.

"Beautiful," Ivy continued softly. She cleared her throat. "What's *your* name?"

The Skullstalker was silent for so long that Ivy thought she'd offended him. But before she could apologize, his fanged mouth opened.

"Vale," he said gruffly. He sounded surprised, like he hadn't expected her to ask.

"Vale," Ivy repeated, sinking into a deep curtsey. "It's an honor to meet you."

The Skullstalker—*Vale*—said nothing. Ivy sweated, staring down at her bare feet. Did she displease him? Maybe he would eat her after all.

He won't need to, she reminded herself. *Not if you prove you're worth keeping.*

For a month, at least. Then the Circle of the Jeweled Fist would come back for her. And more importantly, him. But only if she did what she came here to do.

Ivy straightened and gave Vale her best smile, which was

admittedly still lacking. "What would you have me do first? Whatever you need, I'll do it!"

This didn't make him happy either. If anything, Vale only looked annoyed.

"I suppose I will show you to the eastern rib-thickets," he said slowly. "They grow new bones every day."

"Bones?" Ivy asked faintly.

Vale lifted his head to the shimmering sky. "You will not find your mortal plants here. Will this disturb you?"

"No," Ivy said, too fast. "Like I said, I love plants! Even if..."

She trailed off, her gaze catching on yet another decaying frog. Despite what the rot might suggest, it was happily climbing a strange, bony tree trunk.

Before she could assure her new master of her devotion to these nightmarish plants, a sharp, bulbous jawbone on the end of a vine darted out of a nearby bush and swallowed the rotting frog whole.

Ivy couldn't help it: she shrieked.

Vale didn't react in the slightest as the vine slid back into the bush, pulling its chewing jawbone with it.

"If you cannot handle this work," he began.

"I can handle it!" Ivy blurted, heart racing. She needed to do this *now*. She might not get a chance otherwise.

She patted her dress, ignoring the vial her uncle had sewn into the side. "Oh, no! I-I must have dropped my ring in all the fuss. It's my uncle's, the only thing he gave me to remember him by! I need to retrace my steps and look for it... Please, I beg you, give me two minutes to search!"

Vale's tail flicked in annoyance. Ivy waited, sweat dampening her bloodied dress. He had taken the time to heal her wound. Surely, he didn't want to eat her before she had *proven* that she was unable to do the work?

"I'll come straight back," Ivy blurted. "Then I will serve you with all I am. I swear!"

Vale's face betrayed nothing. The part she could see, anyway. She wished she could see under the skull mask, but she suspected it would be just as expressionless as his mouth.

"You are very dedicated," he said finally. "Would you truly sacrifice the rest of your years to toil in a Skullstalker void for your people?"

Ivy startled. Was that a *compliment*? She couldn't tell. He didn't sound impressed, just... curious.

Ivy tried to come up with something to say. Nothing came to her. She had been so busy obsessing over the plan, she had never thought about why she was doing it.

"My uncle asked me to," she said finally.

It sounded mortifyingly childish. But it seemed enough for Vale, who stood motionless for several agonizing seconds before inclining his head.

"Two minutes," he said. "Hurry. Mortals do not have enough time to waste."

"Oh! Thank you!" Ivy sank into a clumsy curtsey and rushed off, sprinting back through the dense bush. For a moment, she relied on plants she recognized from their walk—a bush made from grasping hands, a tree dripping with spikes. Then she noticed something on the ground.

Footprints. Dark and wispy, emanating shadow into the air. She was *sure* she hadn't left footprints earlier. But here they were, leading her back.

Ivy ran faster, her dress sticking to her slick skin. Was the void leading her into a trap? Was it all a trick, and the Skull-stalker would be waiting for her at the pool, ready to devour her?

The wispy footprints ended at the silver pool they had surfaced from. Ivy looked around wildly, but no Skullstalker was watching. No heavy footsteps behind her.

Ivy bit her lip. Then she grabbed the bloody section of her dress, ripping open the secret pocket she'd sewn shut this morning and fishing out a vial. She uncorked it, careful not to get any of the viscous pale liquid on her fingers. Then she dropped the vial into the silver pool. It bobbed twice, then sank.

For a moment, nothing happened. Ivy's heart fell, and she imagined being truly trapped in this void for all her years, never seeing her uncle again, failing the Circle—

The silver pool began to froth. Pale liquid bubbled up to the surface, the vial's contents emptying into the pool from underneath the surface.

The silver pool roared to a boil. But just as fast as it started, the liquid settled. All was calm. The pool looked like it had when Ivy had stepped out of it.

Ivy fiddled nervously with her bloody dress. Would this be enough to weaken the void? Would it be enough to weaken Vale? Her uncle had assured her it would be. That poisoning the portal would, in turn, poison the void, weakening the Skullstalker enough to control him when the time came. But it had never been done before. How could he be sure if it had never been done?

She had faith in her uncle. They needed more than a Skullstalker's horrific plants to reclaim their place in the palace; they needed a *Skullstalker*. One month from now, the portal would be so weak that the Circle could march right in and bind him.

Ivy just had to buy time until then. If she was killed before the month was up—by Vale or by his brutal, beautiful void—it would all be worth it. She had done what she came here to do. It was all worth it for the Circle, and for her uncle.

So why did she so desperately want to live?

Ivy shivered and turned back the way she'd come. Time to reunite with her new master and convince him she was worth keeping around.

She only made it two steps before something caught her eye.

A rose. Sitting right next to the pool, so large and red, she didn't know how she hadn't noticed it before. Its petals were lush and shiny, the only spot of red in the dark forest. And it reminded Ivy of something... What was it?

The scent hit her then, washing any attempt at remembering away. Ivy gasped in shock. It was *gorgeous*. The best thing she'd ever smelled. She had to get closer.

She swayed toward the rose, narrowly avoiding stepping into the silver pool as she leaned in. The rose was even more perfect up close. And something was swelling at the center...

Ivy didn't have time to wonder what it was before it burst. Golden dust exploded in her face.

Ivy stumbled back, coughing. She was *covered* in it, gold dust dripping from her circlet braid and sticking to her dewy cleavage. It was even in her mouth, tickling her throat as she coughed.

Something growled behind her.

Ivy whirled, still wheezing. Vale loomed behind her, so silent she was sure that he'd seen her poison the pool. Surely now he would eat her.

"You have been sprayed by a heatbloom," Vale snapped, annoyed. "This might delay our work."

Ivy coughed and rasped, "I can still—"

He cut her off. "How do you feel?"

Ivy coughed again, wiping at her face. "What? I feel—"

She stopped. She felt *hot*. Fever-hot. But there was something else: a feeling. An emotion that didn't belong to her. Deep, incandescent joy. Like she had met someone she had been waiting for her whole life.

Then it was gone. It happened so fast she thought she must've imagined it.

"Mortal," Vale prompted.

Ivy blinked hard. Her vision fuzzed, sweat breaking out across her cleavage, sending fat drops of gold-dusted sweat into her dress.

"I—" Ivy said, and stared down at the gold dust in fear. "What is this going to *do* to me?"

"I do not know," Vale admitted, irritated. "I have never seen its effects on a mortal before."

He ran his tongue distractedly over his fangs, and for a strange moment, Ivy was entranced. She wanted his tongue on her, around her, *inside* her—

Vale picked her up. He did it so easily, just like before, and Ivy had to stop herself from gripping his big arms and squeezing. What was *wrong* with her? Why was she suddenly lusting after a monster?

"Where are we going?" she slurred as the Skullstalker set off through the forest.

"To my nest," Vale replied.

Three

Vale had not used his nest in a long time.

He required so little sleep, after all. And the void kept him eternally busy. If bushes didn't part for him to walk through, he would not be able to remember where his nest was.

"This place is wonderful," Ivy mumbled as yet another bone-bush moved out of the way for them. "Scary. But *wonderful.*"

Vale ignored her. He stepped past the bone-bush, eyeing it curiously. The void had not been so *responsive* in centuries. Last year—or possibly several years ago—he had fallen off the top of a tall tree, and nothing had moved to break his fall. Now everything twisted and snapped out of his way like it was easy.

Ivy's head lolled against his robed chest, all the fear gone from her scent. Courtesy of the heatbloom, Vale reminded himself as she smudged her flushed, pollen-streaked cheek against his robe. He could already smell it taking effect, hot desire rising off her skin. At least she was doing her best to ignore it, none of the moaning or begging that he had expected.

Perhaps it did not affect mortals as much as it did demons or other paranormal creatures who took the pollen recreationally. The last thing he wanted was a heat-struck mortal in his void.

"Did that rose have feelings?" Ivy asked suddenly.

Vale did not know what a "rose" was. He assumed it was whatever mortal plant the heatbloom had transformed into to lure her in. It was gone by the time he showed up, using the cover of gold pollen to retreat into the undergrowth.

"Feelings," he repeated.

Ivy nodded, her eyes half-lidded with pollen fever. "I felt this incredible *joy* when it sprayed me. It wasn't mine; I could tell. Was it the rose?"

Vale frowned down at her. He had assumed she was delusional from the heatbloom pollen. But this sounded like something else. Something he previously thought was impossible.

"Everything in this void is connected," Vale admitted grudgingly. "Do you still feel it? The emotion that does not belong to you?"

"No," Ivy sighed. "It was so odd. Like I was... *connected* to something."

Another bush moved out of the way, its bony leaves clacking. Vale glared at it, waiting for an explanation. But nothing pulsed into him—no whisper, not even a fleeting emotion. Once, he was so attuned with the void they were practically one and the same. Now it was communing with this *mortal*? Even his long-dead light-mote assistants had lived longer than mortals, who died within the century. What was the point?

Another hot flush of desire rose from Ivy's skin. Vale closed his mouth, trying not to breathe it in. He could not afford to get distracted.

Ivy struggled against his grip, panic seeping back into her scent. "I can— I can work. You said something about... bone thickets?"

"The eastern rib-thickets," Vale agreed. "They have been extremely unwieldy."

"*Extremely unwieldy*," Ivy whispered. Then she giggled, and the noise reminded Vale of a noise the light-motes used to make when they were happy. He had forgotten.

"They didn't say you would be like this," Ivy mumbled. "Said... said you were only knowledgeable when it came to killing. You sound like a scholar."

Vale did not bother replying. Largely because he had no interest in what was being said, also he did not know what a scholar was.

Ivy lifted her head. There was a gold mark on his robes where her soft cheek had been resting.

"If you eat me," she said, her voice very small, "could you do it fast?"

"I will not eat you," Vale said, annoyed. "I told you, I am *very* badly in need of an assistant."

"What if I'm bad at it?" Ivy croaked, her scent jumbled with a confusing blend of desire and mourning. "The palace gardeners always said I was getting in their way. And once I mistook a bad mushroom for a good one, and I made the whole Circle sick for weeks."

"I will not eat you until you have proven yourself utterly useless," Vale assured her. "And with training, you will not be. Are you satisfied?"

He looked down at her, expecting to see her relax. But if anything, she was only more upset.

"You seem nice," she whispered. Tears glistened in the corners of her eyes.

Vale did not understand her. If she was worried about being eaten, why should he upset her by being *nice*?

The last bone-bush splintered out of his way. Vale stepped into a familiar clearing, his tail unfurling in relief as he saw his nest stacked in the middle.

It had a base of bones, naturally. Then a cover of vines, for comfort. Finally, a layer of fur stripped from the nightbeasts. The fine sheen of cobwebs was new, and they vanished with a sweep of his robe.

Ivy sat up, wiping pollen from her eyelids. Her circlet braid had fallen from her head, her crimson crown turned into a limp line over her shoulder.

"Where are we?"

"My nest," Vale explained. He lowered her into it, surprised by how small she looked inside it. Small and *soft*, her plump body was an oddly satisfying addition to the lush fur lining his nest.

"You will stay here until the heatbloom is out of your blood," Vale continued.

"But," Ivy started, pushing herself up on trembling elbows. "I'm meant to be of use."

Golden pollen pooled between her breasts. Vale's gaze dropped to it, unable to stop himself.

Ivy gasped, her red cheeks flushing even further. Vale could smell the heat between her legs, sweet and tantalizing.

Vale looked away, ignoring the strange stirring in his stomach. Hunger, of course. He wanted to sink his fangs into her soft thigh. But he also wanted to pry her legs open and taste her in a way that had nothing to do with how long it had been since his last meal.

He frowned, examining the pollen on his robes. Usually, all filth slid off him effortlessly. Was the heatbloom affecting him, too? Impossible. He had touched this pollen a hundred times over the years. It had never done anything to him before. He did not feel feverish, just... surprisingly interested in the mortal lying in his nest.

"Um," Ivy squeaked, pulling at her bloodstained dress. "Wh-what did you say this pollen did again?"

"I did not," Vale said. He concentrated, willing the pollen off his robes. Most of it tumbled off, but faint stains remained.

He glared at his surroundings resentfully. Bone-bushes and

trees would bend backwards to allow him to pass, but they would not clean his robes? What was happening to his void?

For the first time in a long time, the void answered. At least, it tried to. Bony branches coiled up his leg, throbbing in alarm.

"*Now* you speak with me," Vale muttered.

"The plant spoke to you?" Ivy said weakly. "What did it say?"

"The plant said nothing," Vale corrected. "The void is attempting to commune."

The bony branches were retreating, a path clearing back where he had come from. Showing him where to go, yet again.

"Stay here," Vale told Ivy.

Ivy struggled to her feet. "What? No! I'll come."

"You should rest."

"It's not that bad," Ivy insisted, clearly lying. She was sweating hard, desire wafting off of her in waves.

She wobbled toward the edge of the nest. Vale considered restraining her, then decided against it. The void had obviously taken a liking to her for some incomprehensible reason. It would not harm her.

Vale set off down the path that the void had cleared for him. Interestingly, it led him straight back to the silver pool. He stood in front of it, annoyed.

"You might have told me when I was here mere minutes ago," he said aloud. "I carried the mortal all the way back. What was the point?"

The void gave no answer.

Ivy stumbled behind him, panting. She was so unsteady on

her feet that Vale almost regretted making her walk. He had hoped she would give up and head back to the nest.

"The void will not harm you, even if you are left alone," he said reluctantly. "You should have..."

He trailed off. Something was pulsing inside the pool.

He stared into its silvery depths. The pool throbbed thrice more, then something he had never seen before happened:

A white crack appeared in the ground.

The air shivered. For the first time in decades, Vale felt what the void was feeling.

Fear. Deep dread. Something was poisoning it.

Then the void left his mind, and Vale reeled. *Poisoning* his void? There was only one explanation, whether she was aware of it or not...

He turned to Ivy. "Did you find your ring?"

Ivy blinked rapidly. There was no sour guilt in her scent, only the heady desire that was becoming difficult to ignore.

"My..." She touched her finger, where a ring might have rested. "No. But—but it showed me footprints. Back to the pool. Do you think it's in there?"

A hundred possibilities flashed through Vale's mind: a cursed ring crafted to poison the pool as he carried her into his void. Or perhaps the ring was just an excuse to come back here with whatever magical horror she had been hiding.

Vale turned his face to the dark, shimmering sky and waited.

No answer came. But no vines came shooting out of the ground to ensnare Ivy, no bones forming a cage to trap her inside. If she were truly a threat, the void would tell him.

Especially since it was so *talkative* now.

Ivy peered at the crack next to the pool. "Is that bad?"

"Yes," Vale admitted. "Something has happened to the pool. Whatever happens to the pool will affect the entire void. I must contact my brother before it worsens."

"Your *brother*?" Ivy whirled on him, the movement so fast it made her stumble. She grabbed his robed arm, her fingers sinking into the muscle underneath. Ivy trailed off, staring at his arm in a way he had not been looked at in a very long time. The scent of desire thickened, and Vale was appalled to realize it was not entirely coming from her.

Calm yourself, he thought. He extracted his arm from her hold, and Ivy gasped as if coming up for air.

"Your... brother," Ivy repeated, wiping her sweaty hair from her face. "Is it the one who took a sacrifice centuries ago and made her a god?"

Vale held back a rare laugh. Mortals lived such short lives that these stories got distorted over mere centuries.

"Ruby was never a sacrifice," he said. "And she made *herself* a god."

He moved to step into the pool.

"Wait!" Ivy cried. "Take me with you."

She stepped toward the edge of the pool, near the crack in the ground. He caught her arm, moving her away.

"Go back to your nest," he said, and frowned. "*My* nest."

"But I'm sick! I don't know what's happening to me. And I don't..." Ivy grimaced, as if revealing something she was deeply ashamed of. "I don't want to be alone."

For a moment, Vale was almost regretful that he had to leave. But he was not about to let her into his brother's void—what if she accidentally poisoned that void, too? If it was not a dissolving ring or some other mysterious object, then it was her body itself. Likely another plot from her uncle, binding his niece to corrupt any void she entered.

"I will only be a moment," Vale said. "Go back to your—my —*the* nest. The way is clear."

He motioned toward the path that the void had cleared for them. But when he stepped into the silver pool, Ivy was still staring mournfully down at him, stinking of panic and lust, a distracting line of sweat dripping between her heaving breasts.

Vale emerged into the wanderer's void with a grateful gasp of fresh air. No fear clouding it, no desire conjured from the heat-bloom. Just the familiar earthy scent of his eldest brother's void, which also hosted a shadowy forest. Just without all the "interesting additions," as his brother called them. It looked positively empty compared to the cramped jungle of Vale's own void.

A surprised voice sounded behind him. "Vale! What brings you here?"

Vale turned. His brother's wife, Ruby, strode through the trees, her dark dress trailing behind her.

"Ruby," Vale said. "I must speak to my brother."

"He's guiding a sprite out of the void," Ruby said, her hair shining in the sunlight that did not exist for many centuries before she made the wanderer's void her home. "I'm sure he'll be here as soon as he senses you."

Slate, the oldest of all known Skullstalkers, appeared beside his wife in a cascade of shadows. He wore age well, only the barest signs tracing his skull mask and thinning his claws. He wore a simple loincloth, as most Skullstalkers did, though his was now embroidered on one side with his wife's spiraling blue embellishments.

"Vale," Slate said, surprised. "You smell... concerned."

His tone was pointed. He could smell the lust on him, Vale realized with a stab of annoyance. Some of it was even his own.

"I was summoned into the mortal realm," Vale said, deciding not to explain that part just yet. "They offered me a mortal in exchange for fodder for their war. But when I brought the mortal into my void, it began showing signs of corruption. Do you know how to fix this?"

"I do not," Slate said slowly. "I have never heard of such a thing. You think the mortal is involved?"

"I do. But..." Vale growled. "My void has... taken a liking to her."

"A *liking*," Ruby repeated, her eyes glinting with god-light. "And here I thought even your void has barely taken a liking to you in the last few centuries! What's so special about her?"

"Nothing," he said hastily. "I only mean that she must have a good heart if my void likes her."

"But that does not mean she did not do something *unknowingly*," Slate said.

Vale nodded. "It may be a plot contrived by the other mortals."

"You could return and kill them," Slate suggested.

Ruby gave her husband a disapproving look. Slate noticed it and sighed.

"You could *ask* them," he amended. "And then kill them if they mean to harm your void."

Ruby patted Slate's arm and turned back to Vale. "Whatever the problem is, I'm glad you are not alone anymore."

Vale frowned. Ruby made it sound like this was a lasting arrangement.

"She is a mortal," he said. "She will die soon enough. Sooner than the light-motes, even."

The memory of his light-mote assistants made his heart throb. He had not thought of them so often in centuries, their sweet light and friendly song. Memories of better times, back when the void and he were one. Back when he was not constantly busy keeping it content, losing more ground every day.

"She doesn't have to die," Ruby said brightly. "I'm still around, aren't I?"

"Because you are a god," Vale said, confused.

"That didn't give me as many years as my dear husband." Ruby ran a fond hand over her husband's claws as he wrapped an arm around her shoulders. "You have a brother in the Anderfel mountains, in the mortal realm. He has a spell that can link your lifelines together."

"I will consider that," Vale lied. He hardly knew this mortal;

he was not about to bind them together for the rest of his life. "I must go. I will seek out the mortals who gave her to me and demand answers. If it is a mortal spell, it will not be too difficult to figure out."

He began to close his eyes and concentrate on his own void. But before he let it pull him under, he paused.

"We have a plant in my void," he began. "The heatbloom. Have you heard of it?"

"The mating plant?" Slate's gaze dropped to the spots of pollen on Vale's usually spotless robe. Then he chuckled, a noise so rare Vale had not recognized it the first time he heard it from his brother's fanged mouth. "Of course I have."

"Do you know how it affects mortals?"

"The same way it affects any creature, I would imagine."

Vale growled again, the sound rising in the silent forest. "This is different. She said she was *connected* to something."

"Her desires," Ruby guessed.

"No. I think... I think it may have been my void. But that is impossible."

"Why?"

"It would not reach out to her," Vale argued. "It barely reaches out to *me*, the one who has cared for it for millennia. Why would it connect with a mortal after mere minutes?"

Ruby and Slate traded a look. Slate's tail flicked. Ruby flicked her hand back at him, a silent conversation that Vale did not understand.

"You should return," Slate said. "Your mortal needs you."

"She is not *my* mortal," Vale replied.

"Still," Ruby said, oddly sweet. "Do let us know how she is. And you may want to visit your Anderfel brother first."

"If I am to go to the mortal realm, it will be to confront the mortals who provoked this situation," Vale said. "Not to extend my new assistant's life."

"He does not only extend her life," Ruby said, her dark hair swelling with magic as she got more excited. "He can also help with the... size problem."

Vale said nothing. His mind filled with images of the small, plump human waiting for him back in his void. Her flushed cheeks and needy words, which would surely be needier as the heatbloom sank into her blood. *Help with the size problem?* How, by causing him to shrink? That seemed like the only way he could mate with her.

"You need not worry," Slate assured him. "Neither of you will be changed. Not permanently."

"And it will not hurt," Ruby added.

Vale shifted uncomfortably, glad for his long robes. They hid the stirring happening underneath. He had not seriously considered mating her, even as the pollen took hold. He still hoped that it would resolve itself some other way, or that she would suffer in silence. But if she was truly beloved by the void—no matter how nonsensical it was—then he owed it to her, did he not? Even if she was just an assistant who the void ignored, as it largely ignored him. She did not deserve the agony that set in if the pollen was ignored.

"Do let us know how it goes," Ruby said again, smiling far too excitedly.

Vale nodded. Then he closed his eyes, concentrating on his void.

It pulled him home in an instant.

The silver pool felt... *off*. The water stuck to him for a moment before sliding away, as all filth did in his void.

Well, Vale thought grudgingly. *Almost everything.*

He wiped fruitlessly at the pollen stains on his robe and then examined the evidence of the pool's corruption. The crack next to the pool was bigger, carving jagged white lines into the dark ground.

Vale would visit the mortal realm again, he decided. They could not have gone far. He would track them down and then demand answers.

But before he could close his eyes again, something landed on his arm.

He looked down. There was a corpsefrog clinging to his robe, watching him with calm, glowing eyes.

"Hello," said Vale suspiciously. "What do you want?"

The corpsefrog let out a low, broken cry. Then it leapt onto a nearby rib-tree, which bowed under its weight. As Vale was puzzling how a tiny corpsefrog could cause such a thing, a surge of bone-trees and bushes parted to show the way back to his nest, including the tree the frog was sitting on.

Vale sighed. "You would have me go to her?"

There was no reply. Not even the corpsefrog, who was still

watching him with those big, glowing eyes, one of which was half-rotted.

"I should return to the mortal realm," Vale said. "Surely that is more important. You are hurting."

Still no reply. Not even a gust of wind. But just as Vale was about to instruct the pool to take him to the mortal realm, a faint moan echoed through the branches.

Vale stopped. The sound should not have affected him. The desire came anyway, pulsing through him in a way he had not known in an age. The strange thing was, it did not *feel* like the pollen was affecting him. He was not overheated or dazed. But it must have been the pollen, for why else would he find himself so drawn to the mortal's desperate moans?

Vale stepped out of the pool and started down the path the void had cleared for him. The mortal's moans became louder with every step, as if she could sense him coming. But when he arrived at his nest, Ivy's eyes were clenched shut, oblivious to his presence.

Her white dress had been pulled up. Her hand was underneath it, rubbing between her legs. Her expression was pained, as he hoped it would not be. But, apparently, the heatbloom worked in the usual way for mortals, too.

The scent of her desire was so thick that Vale was lightheaded with it. He forced his voice to stay neutral as he asked, "Have you made yourself come?"

Ivy jolted. Her hand stopped, her eyes flashing open, and Vale was once again entranced by the bright, familiar green.

"What?" Ivy managed. A shudder wracked her frame, and

Ivy whined weakly. Her hand moved under her dress once more, only to forcefully stop as she stared up at him.

Vale stepped closer, breathing through his mouth so he would not be affected by the overwhelming scent of her desire. "Have you?"

"Yes," Ivy whispered, her cheeks red with more than lust. He could smell her embarrassment, but her desire was so huge it was difficult to notice.

"Then clearly it is not enough," Vale decided. "I will assist."

Four

Huh, Ivy thought feverishly. *I guess I'm seducing him after all.*

She should be terrified. She had a Skullstalker skulking toward her, a sight that most mortals didn't survive. But the pollen made her only focus on the parts of him that intrigued her—his height, his toned muscles bulging against his robe, his intense gaze. She even wanted to run her fingers through the moss growing over his cheekbone. To touch the tips of his fangs. To—

Another wave of heat ran through her, making her shudder against the nest. Whatever this monster was going to do, she needed it *now*.

Still, Ivy's survival instincts weren't *completely* dormant.

"Can we even—" Ivy asked weakly, pulling her dress back down with shaky hands. "I mean... you're not even *human*."

"I will not mate you properly," Vale assured her.

Disappointment and relief rushed through Ivy in equal measure. She dug her fingers into the fur that coated the nest. "But you said—"

"I will assist," Vale repeated. Then, in a move that made Ivy's breath catch, he climbed onto his knees.

He was still huge like this. Still loomed over her, that piercing gaze fixed on her in a way that reminded her eerily of a mouse being stalked by a fox.

"You do not need to fear," Vale said as he leaned closer. "I will take care of you. The pollen will leave your blood. And then we can get back to work."

"Oh," Ivy squeaked. "Um. Okay."

She wanted to say something about how she didn't expect a Skullstalker to be such a dedicated worker. But he gripped her legs, and his touch forced everything from her mind that wasn't primal excitement.

His claws pricked through her dress. For some reason, this only made Ivy more excited, her hips bucking without her consent.

"S-sorry," she stuttered. "I can't stop it."

Vale didn't reply. He pushed her dress up, and Ivy was surprised to see genuine hunger in the slack line of his jaw. She hoped it was *metaphorical* hunger, but she couldn't tell with all his robes hiding... whatever equipment he had down there.

Ivy bit her lip, still self-conscious even with the pollen raging through her. In terms of seduction, this was possibly the best-case scenario. She was awful at seduction, a fact she tried to convince her uncle of, to no avail. But her uncle told her to do it, and so she had reluctantly agreed.

He would be proud of me, Ivy thought, and then had to immediately stop thinking of her uncle. Just as he had purposefully shied away from any graphic detail when he was urging her to "do whatever it took" to make the Skullstalker attached to her, both of them had avoided each other's eyes as he talked in confusing metaphors.

Vale pushed her thighs apart. Ivy let him, legs shaking despite the desire surging through her. His fangs were so *sharp*. What was he going to do?

Another pulse of hot desire flooded through her, a lance of pain following it. Ivy cried out, her fingers twisting in the fur-lined nest as the pain took over.

Then something soft and slick touched her thigh, and the pain subsided.

Ivy looked down. Vale's tongue was sliding up her leg, so long and pink it made her gasp. It ran through the slick on her thighs—evidence of what the pollen was doing to her—and a strange rumbling noise emerged from Vale's throat.

Not quite a growl. It was almost... a purr?

Those dangerous fangs did not come close to her leg, only his long, otherworldly tongue. It moved closer to her hole, brushing her folds so gently that Ivy gasped.

"You're—" Ivy panted. "Are you going to—?"

Vale's tongue drew back, and Ivy whimpered in protest.

"You need something inside you," Vale explained. "This will suffice."

Then his tongue was on her again, licking a line up her folds and grazing her clit. Ivy keened, one hand leaving the fur-covered nest to wrap around one of his antlers.

Both of them froze.

Ivy squeaked, letting go of the antler like it had burned her. "Sorry! I'm—I'm—*ah*!"

Another wave of pain cascaded through her. Then Vale's tongue started to move again, and the pain vanished.

Ivy returned her hand to the fur, her heart hammering. She hadn't been thinking, too caught up in the pollen. She wouldn't do it again. No matter how much she suddenly wanted to touch those strange, barbed antlers. This wasn't for his pleasure, she reminded herself. It was so she could finally get to work.

Vale's hot, wet tongue pressed inside her hole. The first brush was surprisingly tentative, and through the haze of pollen-lust, Ivy was surprised. Then his grip tightened on her legs, and his tongue pushed forcefully inside.

Ivy jerked, her mouth falling open. It was too much—of course it was, it was a Skullstalker's inhumanly long tongue. It was too big, too thick, pressing against her walls before they were ready to let him in. It ached to the point she worried he would tear her.

And yet Ivy's hips moved on their own accord, trying to get his tongue deeper.

"Yes," she heard herself moan. "Like that!"

Her hand came up again, instinctively reaching for the

antler she had just pulled back from. But before she could stop herself, something wrapped around her wrist.

She looked over. It wasn't his tail, like she had been expecting. It was a *vine*. This one looked like it was made of shadows, soft clouds wisping over her skin as it held her still with surprising force.

Vale's tongue paused once more. When Ivy looked down, he was watching the vine with an air of... frustration? Ivy had assumed he was the one who ordered it. Just how much was he in control of his void?

"Ridiculous," Vale muttered. Then he lowered his head yet again, and his tongue resumed its rough shove inside her.

Ivy sank her teeth into her lip, letting the pollen roll through her. She felt like she was going insane. She was lying with her dress rucked up, baring herself to a literal *monster*, and it was all she could do not to moan for more. She just wished she could tell if he was enjoying this. Not that she cared, it was just— Well, it was nice to be enjoyed. For a moment, when the vine wrapped around her wrist, she had entertained the idea that he couldn't control himself, that she was distracting him to the point of letting his void run amok.

Another wave of pollen-lust slammed into her, and Ivy cried out, voice breaking with need.

"Please," she babbled nonsensically. "Please, please, *Vale*!"

She tried to grip his antlers. Another vine shot out and coiled around her wrist, holding both her hands down against the fur-lined nest. Then two more vines wrapped around her ankles, pulling her legs apart.

Ivy moaned. She should be even more terrified now, but for some reason, all she felt was exhilarated. Then she got another pulse of borrowed emotion, just like she had when the pollen first showered over her: *joy*. It was so huge and bright she couldn't help but laugh with glee, even as the borrowed emotion faded.

Vale's tongue slid out of her again. Ivy gasped, jogging her hips fruitlessly. When nothing happened, she looked up.

Vale was staring down at her, his glowing green eyes unreadable. Ivy wished she could see under his skull mask. There was only so much she could read from the exposed part of his face.

Vale pressed a retracted claw to the vine tying her left ankle. Ivy twitched in response, wondering if he was picturing the same thing she was. This was the second time she had been tied up and presented to him.

Vale's claws slid out, drawing the vine tight. Ivy waited, trembling with nerves and pollen-lust. Would he cut her free again, like he had done with the ropes her Circle had tied? Or would he continue like this, with Ivy bound and spread out for him to do whatever he wished?

Finally, Vale sighed and let the vine slip free from his claw.

"What a strange gift those mortals gave me," he said, as if to himself.

Ivy started to reply. But the pollen sent another pulse of pain through her, and all that came out of her mouth was a whimper.

"Yes, yes," growled Vale. "You have no patience."

"Sorry," Ivy managed.

"I was not speaking to you," Vale said. He gave the vines around Ivy's limbs one last glare. Then he lowered his head and plunged his tongue inside her, so thick and fast Ivy keened.

It was too much, again. But how *wonderful* it felt to be given more than she could handle. And Ivy was stretching, her walls slowly giving way to Vale's impossibly long tongue. Each thrust went deeper until he was pressing against her limit. And still he thrust, fast and pulsing, letting out a muffled growl as spit dripped down her thighs.

Ivy bucked mindlessly, lost in it. She tried to touch her breasts, but the vines held her back. Somehow, their constant pull only sent her closer to the edge. She had made herself come several times while he was gone, but this felt different. She could feel the pollen inside her: shifting, burning, *expectant*.

"Please," Ivy begged, sobbing with it. "Please, I need— You have to touch me!"

She squirmed and twisted, but it was no use. She could do nothing but lie there while he plundered her, his grip tightening on her thighs and his growls getting louder. He was definitely affected, Ivy realized with the small part of her brain that wasn't shaking apart. She still couldn't tell if it was to fuck her or eat her.

She stared down at him, wishing she could see his cock. Was it big? It had to be; he was massive. She imagined him looming over her, his pretty little offering for him to do what he wished, and bringing out that big, inhuman cock—

One of Vale's not-quite-retracted claws touched her clit. It was sharp, more a graze than a press, but it was enough.

Ivy screamed. The pollen surged through her, molten and all-consuming. The vines pulsed with each wave of pleasure, and Ivy found herself wishing that Vale would cover them with his body, holding her down properly.

Gradually, the pleasure faded enough for Ivy to pry her teary eyes open.

Vale was sitting on his haunches like a dog. His mouth was open, his tongue hanging out as he panted. Then he caught her looking, and his jaw snapped shut, that gorgeous tongue vanishing inside it.

"The pollen," Vale panted, more growl than voice. "Is it gone?"

Ivy pushed her dress down, considering. She was sweating, but it didn't feel feverish like it had before. The desperation was gone. So was the pain. She was dazed and exhausted and still partly expecting to get eaten, but her mind was her own again. No pollen. No emotions that didn't belong to her.

"'S gone," Ivy slurred. She cleared her throat, trying to sit up. The vines tugged on her wrists.

"Oh," Ivy said. "Sorry."

"Do not be," Vale said, sounding annoyed. He stood, brushing off his robes. "It is not you."

With that, the vines retreated. Ivy held up her hands to see a faint red mark around her wrists. Her ankles were also marked, and Ivy felt oddly sad knowing they would fade soon.

She rubbed her wrist cautiously. "That... wasn't you?"

"No," Vale said after a moment. "It was the void."

"The void," Ivy repeated, Vale's words from before running through her head: *the void is attempting to communicate.*

Ivy gasped. "*That's* what's talking to me? The void?"

"The void would not talk to you," Vale said gruffly. "You are new. And *mortal.*"

He said the word with faint disgust. But mostly confusion, as if he was just as baffled as Ivy.

He stared down at the vines that had been holding her down. They were creeping around the nest, Ivy realized with a shock. Like they were waiting to slide back and restrain her again.

"You said it spoke to you," Vale said. "What did it say?"

"It didn't speak. It just..." Ivy straightened her red braid with shaky hands. It was a frizzy mess; she would have to rebraid it later. "It was happy. *So* happy. And..."

She frowned, trying to sift through the hazy memories of her orgasm. There was a moment near the end, so brief she thought she might have imagined it. Even now, it only became clear when she focused. There was something bittersweet under the joy it had shown her.

"It misses you," Ivy realized.

Vale growled louder, the surrounding trees vibrating with the force of it. "I have been here *always.*"

"I'm sorry," Ivy said again, rushed. She bowed her head, but it was difficult to be too frightened. Not with those borrowed emotions echoing through her, as if the connection was still there.

"You used to be content," Ivy said, the words flowing out of her before she could stop them. "You used to love tending to your void. Now it's a chore."

Vale didn't snarl, like Ivy was expecting. He didn't even move. He just stood there, towering over her in a way that should have made her shrink back in terror.

Ivy squirmed, reaching for that strange connection that had given her those words. But it had already faded, just like before. Now all she had were her own thoughts, which were all screaming at her to grovel or run.

Grovel, she decided. Definitely grovel. Running wouldn't help. She was in his void, after all. Even if she suspected it wouldn't hurt her, *he* still could.

But before she could apologize again, Vale turned abruptly.

"I will find the meaning behind this mistaken connection," he spat. "And I will sever it. Do *not* leave my nest."

With that, he vanished into the otherworldly forest. Ivy watched him go, still breathless. She couldn't help but feel like she had done something wrong.

"But I can help," she called through the trees.

No response. Ivy smoothed her sticky dress over her legs, shivering as she felt the combination of her own slick mixing with his Skullstalker drool. Her hand strayed down toward her ankle.

The marks were already fading. Ivy wished she could be sad about it again. But now all she could think of was the chains awaiting Vale when her uncle dragged him out of this void, weak from the poison she had dripped into the silver pool.

For the first time, Ivy wondered what would happen after

the Circle of the Jeweled Fist overthrew the castle. Would they let the Skullstalker—would they let *Vale*—go? Or would they keep him hidden away, captive and controlled? She never spared it much thought until she met him. Everybody said he would be an evil beast. Not this gruff creature who once loved his void so much that it loved him back.

Something brushed her reddened wrist. Ivy yelped, looking over to see yet another vine. It didn't grab her this time. It just nudged her, then retreated.

"What?" Ivy asked shakily. "What do you want?"

The vine nudged her again, then retreated. Behind it, the foliage parted to form a path.

Ivy curled her arms nervously around her knees. "But he said to stay here! I've already gotten myself into enough trouble for one day."

Another nudge. This one was in her head, coaxing and gentle.

Come, it whispered. *You will not displease him.*

Ivy twisted to stare into the woods where Vale had disappeared. Then back to the path the void had made for her.

Another nudge. *You said you wished to help.*

Ivy stared into the woods for a moment longer. When no angry Skullstalker came charging out to roar at her, Ivy took a deep breath and climbed cautiously out of the nest.

Five

The mortals had moved on.

Vale attempted to track them, to no avail. They had used a smelling salt that masked their scent, which only increased his suspicions that they had done something to Ivy before presenting her as an offering.

He retreated to his void and stepped out of the silver pool, gritting his fangs. The crack in the ground was already deeper, creeping toward the base of a bone-tree.

Vale scraped his foot claws against the crack and growled. "Whether she meant to or not, the mortal has done this to you. To *us*! And you still waste your time communing with *her*? She will wither and die within two blooms of a bonetithe plant!"

The void did not answer. Not even a gust of wind curled comfortingly around his antlers.

Vale's growl turned into a roar. Skeletal birds took flight

from trees, and animals scurried through the undergrowth, but Vale could not bring himself to care. He had cared for this void —*his* void—his entire existence. And now it was ignoring him so it could talk to a mere mortal who had been here less than a day.

"Have I displeased you?" he demanded. "She tells me you want me to be *joyous*. How can I be joyous when there is no time to rest? No time to do anything but tend to you! I used to have assistants! What would you have me do? Rest and let you rot?"

The crack in the ground swelled, horrible and pale in the dark soil.

Vale growled at it again. Even raging, he was still worried about it. His void was all he had ever known. He did not want it harmed. Especially considering how closely he was tied to it. If the wilderness void died, so did he.

"The pollen is only meant to awaken her desires," Vale continued. "Not awaken her to *you*. What have you done?"

No response. Even when Vale closed his eyes to listen, the noises that came back were not for him: a root-deer munching; a wooden branch scratching against its bony twin; a shocked, disbelieving giggle.

His eyes snapped open. It was the mortal. And she was *not* in his nest.

Vale snarled and started toward the noise. Her laughter grew closer, and he ignored the sweet taste of her still in his mouth. He made sure the pollen would leave her blood, then she could finally start their work. It did not matter how soft her thighs were under his claws, or how prettily she flushed.

He burst through the bushes to find Ivy stretching to pull a mess of strangling rib-thickets from a tree trunk.

"What are you doing?" Vale demanded.

Ivy gasped and whirled. Her braid had been unspooled, her blazing red hair arcing out so brightly it made Vale's claws clench.

"I'm sorry," Ivy said, twisting a stray rib-bone in her hands. "I— You— The void guided me! It said I could start working like you want me to. I feel better, I promise."

Vale eyed her suspiciously. She was still sweating, but that could be from her work. He sniffed the air. No trace of that hot, sweet scent that was still tantalizing the back of his throat.

Vale ignored the stirring under his robes and demanded, "What were you laughing at?"

"Just…" Ivy motioned at the ground. For the first time, Vale noticed the shadowy vine curling gently around her foot. The same way it had curled around the light-motes when they were alive. The same way it used to curl around his antlers, back when it still spoke to him.

Vale ground his fangs together, his tail lashing. He wanted to roar at the mortal, to berate her again for leaving the nest. But deep down, he knew he would not truly be yelling at her. He would be yelling at the void. This mortal might be clumsy, disobedient, and even infuriating—but she meant well.

Even if she *had* accidentally poisoned his void. He could not fault her for the other mortal's doings.

"We should start at the eastern rib-thickets," Vale gritted, forcing his tail to still. "They are the worst. These can wait."

Ivy blinked in surprise. "Oh! Okay."

After a moment of uncertainty, she threw the broken rib into a pile with the other discarded bones she had been prying off the tree trunk. Then she straightened her dress, blushing as her hands brushed over sodden fabric.

"I'll go wherever you lead me," she said with a nervous smile.

Vale held his breath. That hot scent was in the air again, no doubt agitated by her swishing her dress about. He could not afford to get distracted.

"Come," he said, turning toward the eastern rib-thickets. "We have wasted enough time today."

"Of course," Ivy said.

A weak gurgle echoed through the trees. At first, Vale could not identify it. Then he realized what it was: the soft noise of a mortal stomach growling.

Vale turned back to find Ivy rushing after him, faltering when she saw him stop.

"What is it?" Ivy asked, tugging at her loose red hair. "What's wrong?"

"You," Vale replied, unable to keep the irritation out of his voice. "Did you not eat before you came?"

"Well... yes." Ivy started braiding her hair, her fingers slipping distractedly on the tangled strands. "But it's been, um, a tiring day."

Vale sighed. Ivy startled, and Vale noticed how much his

sigh sounded like a growl. Actually, most of the things that came out of his mouth sounded like a growl. He was so used to it that he forgot that it intimidated most creatures.

Vale asked, "How often do mortals eat?"

"Three times a day," Ivy said reluctantly, as if she were afraid he would disapprove of the answer.

Three times a *day*? Vale sighed again, not bothering to keep the growl out of it this time. His light-motes *never* needed to eat. Why could he not have another assistant like that?

"And snacks," Ivy continued in a whisper.

"And you will need water," Vale said.

"Yes?" Ivy cringed. "I'm sorry."

"It is fine," Vale said grudgingly. "We will find you food and water. You can wash your dress."

"Oh! Now?" Ivy brushed at her dress again, and Vale's fangs snapped shut as he stopped himself from breathing in that hot scent. It was not entirely helpful. Even when he could not smell her, he could still see her flushed cheeks. Her wild crimson hair. Her thin, white dress stuck to her body with sweat. Her nipples pricked underneath the flimsy fabric, her body so soft and ripe—

Vale turned away, forcing down a mouthful of saliva.

"Eat first," he said as he started walking. "Then wash."

He needed to eat, too. It had been weeks, or perhaps months. Soon his own stomach would rumble, and he did not want to see this puny mortal's reaction. It had once caused a visiting sprite to faint in fright.

"Of course," Ivy repeated, her voice small as she hurried after him. "Vale?"

Vale growled, no sigh in it this time. "What?"

She did not reply. Vale whirled and found her standing several feet away, twisting her red hair around her fingers.

"I just wanted to say thank you," she said quietly, eyes on the ground. "You've been good to me. Better than I deserve. I know I've been more trouble than I'm worth."

Vale wanted to snap at her. But she looked so small and defenseless with her useless, blunt teeth and delicate skin. Not to mention the sour scent of guilt underneath the leftover lust drifting up from her damp dress, as if she was ashamed he had to go to the trouble to help her. Vale wondered how they chose her for their "offering." How disposable was she to those people? Even her uncle had been willing to give her up. Vale thought that mortals valued those familial ties.

Maybe they did. But not when it came to the mortal in front of him, her eyes on the ground like she was waiting to be devoured.

Vale thought, for the dozenth time today, of the light-motes. Their cheer and company in between their duties, back when he had time to spare. He used to have visitors in the wilderness void—sprites and nymphs and fellow Skullstalkers. They called him kind, once.

Vale smoothed down his robes, trying to collect himself. "Stay here. I do not care what the void urges you to do. Stay *here*. I will be back with food shortly."

"Yes," Ivy said, flustered. "Thank you, um... Master Skull-stalker."

Vale turned toward his hunting grounds, oddly disappointed. It took him until he was chasing a root-deer to its doom that he realized what the disappointment was: he had been hoping she would say his name.

Vale returned to the spot he had left her in with a dead root-deer slung over his shoulder, its skull-face bumping into his chest with every step.

Ivy stumbled to her feet. A flurry of red flowers fell away from her. Apparently, while he had been gone, she had sat down at the base of a nearby tree, and a layer of unrecognizable flowers had sprouted over her.

"I didn't do it," Ivy said, quickly. "It just happened."

Vale eyed the unfamiliar blooms scattered around her. They smelled rich and sweet, almost sickly. Their red was a near-perfect match to her tangled hair.

"They're roses," Ivy whispered, brushing a petal from her locks. "I'm sorry. I asked the void not to, but they kept growing."

Another "rose" bloomed next to her foot. Ivy nudged it away gently, wincing. Then she pointed at the root-deer draped over his shoulder. He expected her to gasp at its skull-face, but she just smiled.

"Its face is like yours," she said, strangely charmed. "And the antlers."

Vale lifted the dead creature's head. The skull and antlers did indeed match his. They had not when he was first given the wilderness void. But they changed, as did so many things in this void. When he arrived, the root-deer was all roots, and there was no skull to speak of. Then he was given this void, and both he and the animals' forms began to shift to match each other.

"I can prepare it," Ivy continued. "If you'd like."

Vale huffed. "I do not need to prepare it."

"Oh," Ivy said, her eyes widening as she glanced down at his fangs. "That—that makes sense. I can prepare it for myself, then. I won't be a bother."

"We will see," Vale said, perhaps unfairly. He was unusually fatigued after his hunt. He hoped that it was due to how long he had gone without a meal, and not because of the weakening void. Surely it was too early for him to feel those effects.

He hoisted the root-deer further up his shoulder and started into the forest.

"Come," he said again. "You will need a fire."

Ivy scrambled after him. Her footfall was strange. When he turned to check on her, she was stepping over suddenly blooming roses, whispering apologies whenever she accidentally trod on them.

The roses thankfully stopped by the time they found a spot clear enough for a fire. Vale ripped into his half of the root-deer, still disdainful of the mortal's need to cook meat before devouring it. Not to mention Ivy's clear bafflement with the deer he had presented her.

Vale sat up, wiping his bloody mouth with his robe. "What?"

"Nothing," Ivy said hurriedly. She tied the torn deer leg to the stick, then held it over the fire. The meat crisped, the edges turning black in a way that seemed to shock her.

"It's nothing," Ivy said again when she caught him looking. "It's just... is this even *meat*?"

"Of course, it is meat," said Vale. "What else would it be?"

Ivy's nose wrinkled. She poked at the root-deer leg, which dripped bright blood into the fire, throwing sparks. "Um. A... plant? The texture *feels* like fruit, almost. And it looks like fruit. But when I cut into it, it bleeds. And it has bones!"

"Yes. Because it is meat." Vale ripped another hunk of root-deer off its haunches, only chewing twice before swallowing. "Does this displease you?"

"No," Ivy assured him. "I'm sure it will taste wonderful. It *smells* really nice."

She leaned in, sniffing hopefully. Then she pulled the root-deer leg out of the fire and took a small nibble.

Vale waited. "Well?"

"It's nice!" Ivy smiled at him, looking absurdly pleased by the fact. "Thank you."

"You do not have to thank me," Vale said grumpily. "I live to serve. I just never expected to serve my *assistant*."

He wiped his bloody claws on the grass, annoyed. He felt full, but no less tired. A worrying sign.

"You will learn how to live in this void," Vale said. "I will not have to assist you after that. We have too much work to do."

Ivy nodded wildly and bit another tiny chunk out of her deer leg. She was watching him curiously, though she tried to hide it.

Vale growled. "What?"

"Nothing," Ivy insisted. "Just... are you okay? You look different."

Tired, Vale thought. *She means I look tired.*

Luckily, he had been tired for centuries. He knew how to weather it.

"I am well," Vale lied. He ripped another strip of bleeding plant-meat off his deer half, then paused. "And you?"

Ivy blinked in surprise. She was sweating again. Hopefully from the fire. But from the sweet scent wafting faintly off her in a way that had nothing to do with the stains on her dress, Vale doubted it.

However, if Ivy was feeling the pollen's effects again, she did not show it. She smiled again, her soft cheeks gleaming in the firelight.

"I'm fine," Ivy said, avoiding his eyes. "Thank you."

Six

Ivy was *not* fine.

The pollen fever was taking over again. She thought it had "worked its way from her blood," as Vale had put it. But here it was, heating her skin and filling her with want.

Another pulse of lust shot through her, making her gasp. At least, Vale had left her to wash the blood off. He had invited her to join, but Ivy had waved him off and said she was still eating.

Ivy patted the fire out with the remnants of the firewood he had broken off for her and stood. Her vision swam, making her stumble against a tree.

"No," Ivy told herself, as if she could force the pollen to stop from sheer will. "I won't do this again. He already fixed it once. He—he brought me food, and gave me his nest! He's done enough!"

Another explosion of lust burst through her, so intense it made her curl over with a whimper.

Something brushed her bare foot. Ivy looked down to see something strange: an ivy vine studded with roses. Like it had combined her namesake with the rose that pollen plant had lured her in with, the same roses it had showered her with while she was waiting for Vale to come back with the root-deer.

Ivy nudged the ivy-rose vine with her foot. "Are you doing this on purpose? He doesn't even *want* me!"

The strange ivy-rose vine curled around her ankle. At first, Ivy thought it was restraining her, like when she was splayed out in the nest. Then the pressure eased, and Ivy realized it was a strange, thin hug.

Ivy teared up. She didn't want to hurt this place. And the more she spoke to Vale, the less she wanted to chain him. But she would have to move past it, right? For the sake of the Circle.

She pushed away any thoughts of the void, sickened and pale, while her uncle slid an enchanted collar around Vale's neck. Then she straightened and headed for the weak rumble of the waterfall.

It's fine, Ivy assured herself as she walked along the riverbank, strange dark grass tufting between her toes. *You'll stay away. Maybe he won't notice.*

She came to a stop at a pile of black robes.

Vale stood naked under the waterfall with his back toward

her. There were miles of pale blue skin visible above the river water, which only rose to his shins. She could see every inch of his strange, bony back, the barely-there curves of his ass, his strange whippy tail just above it. He should have repulsed her. But she found herself entranced by the water running over his skin, muscles shifting so visibly every time he moved.

Another pulse of heat made Ivy hold back a moan. She squeezed her legs together, as if that would stop the warmth pooling between them. She wanted to touch him so badly. She wanted to feel his hands on her again, those clawed hands curled dangerously around her thighs—

Ivy forced back her thoughts and considered the river. The water *looked* normal enough. Surely it would be okay to wash in.

She gathered her dress, lifting it over her head and forcing herself not to feel self-conscious as the air touched her skin. It was just like bathing with the Circle. Except they usually separated that by gender, unless they were truly desperate.

She waded into the river up to her knees, sighing in relief as the cool water rushed over her flushed skin. Then she dropped her dress in, wishing for soap.

But as soon as she started rubbing at the stains, something strange happened. They vanished. The water carried them out like they were never there.

Ivy held up her sopping dress, shocked. The void *did* like her, she supposed. Apparently, that translated into rivers that washed her clothes as well as the palace staff.

She should have taken the dress back to the riverbank. Started washing the grit and sweat off her own body. But she couldn't stop thinking about Vale, who was under the waterfall just out of view.

She wouldn't look. She *wouldn't.*

Another wave of pollen-heat surged through her. She clapped a hand over her mouth to muffle her moan, but it wasn't enough.

"You need it again," came Vale's gruff voice.

Ivy hugged her wet dress to her front and turned.

Vale was still standing under the waterfall, water streaming down his bare body. But unlike last time, he was facing her.

Ivy couldn't help it: her eyes sank to his cock.

It was big, of course. He was a Skullstalker; it was only proportional. It was human-shaped, and the same pale blue as the rest of him, soft and oddly vulnerable. He had a foreskin, she noted with hazy surprise. She had never seen it in the flesh. Most men in her country had it removed at birth. It filled her with a blazing curiosity to see the cockhead hiding underneath it, foreskin retreating as he hardened—

A low growl dragged her out of her fantasies. Ivy tore her gaze away to see Vale growling, irritated. Her cheeks flushed harder, ashamed. She had annoyed him so much since she arrived, and now she would inconvenience him again?

"You don't need to," Ivy blurted as he stepped out of the waterfall.

"I do," Vale said. "It will kill you otherwise."

Ivy laughed uncomfortably. "Do you care?"

Vale stopped. His tail swished thoughtfully, water dripping down his antlers and through the moss growing on the side of his skull.

"I would not lose the first assistant I have had in centuries," he said slowly. "Get out of the river. Drop your dress."

Ivy shivered. Not from the river, which was no match for her fevered skin. But from his voice, so rough and commanding. The way he loomed over her as he approached, that glowing green gaze fixed so intently on her.

Ivy climbed onto the riverbank and wrung her dress out, then laid it on the strange, dark grass. Everything inside her wanted to lie down and let him do whatever he wanted to her or, failing that, leap into his giant arms. But she held herself back, turning again to face him as he arrived in front of her.

"You don't—" Ivy stopped, gasping as another rush of heat ran through her. "Y-you don't have to."

Vale leaned over her. He was still standing in the river, cool water running around his shins.

"Do you not wish to?"

"No, I just..." Ivy sighed, wiping her stubborn, sweaty hair away from her forehead. "I thought this was done! How many times will it come back?"

"I have never seen a mortal afflicted with it." Vale paused. Then he reached up and pushed away a strand of hair that kept falling into Ivy's eyes, an action that made Ivy's heart stutter in her chest.

Vale blinked rapidly. His hand dropped back to his side, his tail swishing.

"For a demon, it wears off in mere hours," he said, too fast. "But in a mortal's weak blood... I am unsure. Several weeks, perhaps."

"*Weeks*?" Ivy repeated. She couldn't be like this when her Circle barged into this void to take Vale prisoner. What would they say?

"But I can still work," Ivy said desperately. "Right? I can be useful to you? A good assistant?"

Vale said nothing. He stared down at her, and Ivy thought back to being tied up on that stone slab, sure she would be devoured. This felt like that. Only now she *wanted* him to consume her—and in a very different way than he would have back in the mortal realm.

"You can be useful to me," Vale said after a long moment. He blinked hard, as if resurfacing from a daze. "I will try to mate you properly this time. It might give you more of a reprieve between pollen heats."

Ivy's mouth dropped open. She looked down at his naked cock, which, to her terror and joy, was hardening. That gorgeous foreskin worked slowly back, revealing a shiny dark cockhead that made Ivy want to moan. Or better yet, sink to her knees.

She shook her head, clearing the fog. "You'll *try*?"

Vale nodded. "You are very small. I will do my best. Lie down."

Ivy did. It was getting more difficult to think, but she had to cling to the fear before it got buried under the pollen-heat. She couldn't *actually* let him fuck her, right? She'd never taken a cock as big as his. Hells, she'd never *seen* a cock as big as his.

But the pollen was so strong. Any fear she had was drowned out by pure lust, making her whimper.

"Please," she said, her hips lifting off the grass. "Oh, gods. I need it."

Vale reached for her. Then he stopped, watching something to her left.

Ivy turned just in time to watch three shadowy vines creep up to her. They didn't wrap themselves around her wrists, like they had in the nest. Two of them wound around her thighs instead, pulling them open. And the third...

Ivy cried out in shock as the third vine teased her entrance, sliding through the slick that had been gathering there since the second heat struck. She waited to see if Vale would do something, maybe rip the vine away, but he only stood there in the river, watching her with those big, glowing eyes.

"Are you...?" Ivy gasped as the third vine—velvety and oddly warm—pushed ever so gently inside her. "Are you doing this?"

"No," said Vale, sounding surprised. "Can you feel it?"

"Of course, I—" Ivy stopped, her mouth falling open as the vine pressed deeper.

"Through the connection," Vale explained. "Can you feel it?"

Ivy reached for the void through the haze of lust. There, in the very back of her mind, the void was sending her tiny pulses of excitement.

"Yes," she gasped. "It feels... *ohhh*. It feels so strange!"

She laughed giddily, the noise trailing off on a groan as the vine pulsed inside her. Then, to her shock, the vine started to swell.

"Shit!" Ivy tried to close her legs instinctively. But the vines pried them apart again, giving the third vine more space. And in turn, it gave her more space, gently pulsing bigger and bigger, stretching her out.

Vale leaned over her, his tail flicking anxiously. "What is it?"

"It's..." Ivy's eyelids fluttered as the vine pulsed again, shrinking before expanding even bigger than before. "It's getting me ready for you. F-for you to mate me."

Vale's eyes glowed brighter. He climbed onto the riverbank, water sloshing over her bare feet as he crouched over her, his knees digging into the grass near her feet.

He grabbed her legs, dragging her up.

He wants to watch, Ivy realized. She didn't try to close her legs again, but she couldn't help the embarrassment that flooded up underneath the lust as he peered between her legs. The vine was still growing, thrusting in and out with wet noises that made her blush. She almost wished the pollen could turn her mind off entirely, replacing it with animal lust. It would make it easier to let him watch her like this, naked and claimed as the vine fucked into her.

As if it heard her thoughts—which, who knew, maybe it

had—the pollen raced through her again, making her eyes roll back in her head.

"I want it," she heard herself say, her hips working against the vine. She reached down, touching Vale's narrow stomach. "Can I touch it?"

Vale looked up from her stuffed hole. "What?"

"Your—" Ivy had just enough of herself left to be embarrassed to say it. "Your cock. Can I touch it?"

Vale pulled her closer. Ivy's breath hitched as her thighs bumped up against his damp, bony legs, her hand falling easily onto the exposed head of his cock.

Ivy gasped. It *wasn't* human-shaped. Not entirely, anyway. His cockhead was almost flat at the tip, and it was much wider than the rest of him.

She gripped it firmly, entranced. The foreskin ended halfway down his shaft now. She smoothed it back over his oddly shaped cockhead, reveling in the cool, silky texture.

Vale growled, curling over her with his fangs gritted. "Enough. I will mate you now."

The vine inside Ivy swelled so wide she cried out in alarm. It didn't hurt, but it was so close to pain that her hands flew down to still the vine.

Vale grabbed her hands and pinned them to the grass. "It will not harm you. It is too...*fond* of you."

He still sounded confused. Maybe even betrayed. Mostly, he sounded impatient, grinding his huge, cool cock against her thigh where the vine was holding her open.

Ivy bit her lip. "Will *you* harm me?"

"I will do my best not to," Vale replied.

Ivy couldn't help it: she laughed. What else could she do, lying naked and sex-pollened underneath a literal monster who would *try* not to hurt her?

The vine slid out of her. Ivy jerked in shock, her hole squeezing around nothing.

Vale watched the vine retreat.

"Are you done?" he asked the vine. "Do you want another minute with your new favorite person?"

The vine, still slick with Ivy's juices, curled around Vale's antler and squeezed. Then it let go, sliding down to pet Ivy's ankle.

"You are nonsensical," Vale told the vine.

Ivy stared at him, stupidly charmed. There, *finally*, was the creature whom the void loved so much. She could feel its love radiating through her, glad to have him back.

Then Vale pushed his big, flat cockhead into her, and any borrowed love she felt was replaced by a pollen-lust so overwhelming she could do nothing but whimper while it rolled through her.

It ached. Even with the vine stretching her out, his cockhead was too big for her body to take. But it felt too good for Ivy to care. The pollen made her wild, her hips bucking as he slid inside.

Vale grunted, thrusting deeper. After the blunt width of the cockhead, the shaft pushed in shockingly easily. At least, some of it did. When Ivy managed to lift her head, she was dismayed to see that barely a third of his cock was inside her.

Vale grunted, his claws digging into her wrists. "You are so *tight*. I should have let that vine keep mating you."

"Wasn't enough," Ivy gasped. "Want you."

Vale growled and fucked her faster, his flat cockhead bumping into the end of her hole. The wide shape of it dragged deliciously against her insides, making Ivy cry out with each thrust. The pain somehow made it better: the sharp dig of his claws around her wrists; the impossible stretch of his cock; the feeling of his cockhead slamming into the end of her hole like it wanted to fuck through it.

"More," Ivy cried. "Please, more."

But there was no more. Vale could only fit so much of himself inside her. He could push further—of course, he could with all that raw strength—but he didn't. He didn't want to damage her, Ivy realized with shock.

She came like that, her wrists restrained and her hole bruised. The pollen washed over her in a huge, hot rush and then retreated, satisfied.

For now, anyhow.

Ivy's head was clearer now. Less frenzied. She would have expected to be horrified. Instead, she found herself spreading her legs as wide as she could, the vines helping her along as her thighs ached and her hole twinged with each stroke of Vale's brutal cock.

Vale curled over her and froze, trembling. Ivy felt him get even bigger inside her, and then he was gushing, pulse after pulse, until it spilled out around him. Come coated her thighs, dripping over the vines that were holding her legs open.

It went on for an inhumanly long time. Ivy arched to watch him pulse inside her, her mouth watering as she saw the cock stretching her open. She *did* wish he could fit. But the fact that it didn't meant she got to watch his beautiful cock throb with each round he put inside her, come dribbling down her legs to pool in the grass below.

Finally, Vale sagged, his antlers pressing into the ground. Holding himself up, Ivy realized with alarm. He was breathing raggedly, his hands shaking around her legs.

She touched one antler cautiously. It felt like a stupid question to ask a Skullstalker, but...

"Are you alright?"

Vale startled. Ivy wondered when someone last touched him.

"I believe I should be asking you that," Vale said.

He pulled out. Ivy gasped in pain, and this time the vines did not stop her when she closed her legs. One of them—the one that had been inside her, if the sticky residue was any indication—petted her hip comfortingly.

She could feel the void's admiration in the back of her head. It was *proud* of her. It thought she'd done *well*. Ivy couldn't help but tear up at the praise. She couldn't remember the last time someone was proud of her. Even when she agreed to be the Circle's sacrifice, her uncle had only patted her arm and smiled as if it was exactly what he'd expected.

Vale sat up, chest heaving. "Ivy."

"Hmm? Oh! I'm alright." Ivy wiped her eyes and sat up

gingerly, grimacing when it made come gush out of her tender hole. "Sorry."

Vale huffed a noise that was not quite a growl and pushed himself up. It took some effort, both hands braced on the grass so hard he left claw marks.

Ivy frowned. "Are you sure you're okay?"

"The void weakens," Vale said after a moment. "I weaken with it."

Ivy tried to look like this was new information. She didn't need to fake the worry. "What do you mean? What happened?"

"You," Vale said.

The void was still in her head. Ivy tried to push it away, suddenly terrified. If it knew what she'd done, it would tell Vale. He would devour her whole for it, and she couldn't blame him. This void was strange and dangerous, but it shouldn't be poisoned.

She hugged her knees. But before she could beg for mercy, Vale continued.

"You would not know," he said. "My void would not let you stay if you did something to hurt it. Your mortals, however... Did they mention a plan?"

Ivy stared up at him. The wilderness void was still in her head; she could feel it drifting around her skull. It had to *know*. Why not tell him?

"No," she said when the void didn't do anything to alert him. "Just the trade. Me for the weapons."

Vale said nothing for several long moments. Then he

turned, stepping back into the river. With his back toward her, he said, "They must truly believe in their fight to give you up."

Ivy watched him climb further into the river, stunned. His tone was gruff, but his words were so much more than she would expect from a monster she had done nothing but inconvenience from the moment she arrived.

Vale bent down, scooping a handful of water and emptying it over his antlers. It ran down his body in a way that was so distracting, it made Ivy worry the pollen was starting again.

"Come," he said impatiently. "You still need to wash."

Seven

Despite her protests, Vale cleaned the mortal thoroughly before letting her leave the river.

"It is the most efficient way," he insisted as she climbed back onto the riverbank, her legs as shaky as a root-deer sproutling.

Ivy nodded, her cheeks still flushed. "Sure! Um, thank you."

She bent down to gather her dress, which was drying on the riverbank. The grass bent to brush her fingers as she did, and she yelped. It quickly turned into a delighted giggle as the grass wound around her little finger and squeezed.

Vale cocked his head at her. He refused to be charmed by this infuriating mortal. But he would bet that there were not many who would giggle so often in response to the wilderness void's antics. She was coping with her new situation well, even if she kept getting into trouble.

Ivy's dress settled into place over her damp body. She plucked at it, making a face as it settled against her wet breasts.

Vale allowed himself a moment to watch the fabric seal around her firm nipples. Then he averted his gaze and followed her onto the riverbank, scooping her easily into his arms.

Ivy shrieked. It was much quieter than he expected. He ignored it, walking back into the forest. The trees parted for him, and he tried to be grateful rather than annoyed.

"Where are we going?" Ivy asked.

"My nest."

"What?" Ivy struggled against his grip, which was so useless he wondered why she was bothering. "Why? You said you were only doing *that* so I could work!"

"We will work soon," Vale assured her. "Until then, rest. I have something to attend to."

"*You* rest," Ivy protested.

Vale looked down at her. If he was not exhausted, he thought he might be amused. This little mortal, speaking back to him like she had any power over him.

"I mean..." Ivy bit her lip. "Sorry. You said you were tired."

"I have been weary for a long time," he replied. "And I will only get worse now the void has been poisoned."

The last trees parted to reveal his nest. He lowered her into it, pushing her back down when she tried to sit up. Her skin was drier than it should be, much like his own, which was dry as soon as he stepped out of the river to retrieve his robe. So was her dress. And her hair, which fluffed around her in a way that was almost sweet.

"But—" Ivy began.

"Rest," he commanded. "I will be back soon."

He walked toward the silver pool that would take him between voids. The trees did not part for him, and he sighed.

He did not look back. But he felt the mortal's eyes on him until he vanished through the trees.

Slate's void was lit in a strange color, all orange and red. It took Vale a moment to remember what a sunset was. His void was either night or day, with no in between.

He strode through Slate's thin, nonresponsive trees, following his older brother's voice.

"I cannot help you," Slate was saying.

Another voice joined him, deep and raspy. "But... *you* have one."

Slate chuckled.

Vale emerged through the trees. Slate was standing near his nest, talking to a Skullstalker that Vale had never met before. The Skullstalker was smaller, as many younger Skullstalkers were. He had two protruding fangs on his skull mask that were much larger than his natural fangs, and his eyes were huge, the glowing purple pupils fixed pleadingly on Slate as he stared up at him.

"Can you at least tell me how to get one?" the young Skullstalker begged. "Whenever I try, they run away. Even when I tell them I will not eat them!"

"Yes, they do that," Slate said dryly. He noticed Vale, giving him a short nod before returning to the stranger. "I cannot help you with this. You have my sympathies, but stop trying to summon me for this."

With that, he ran a claw down the air between them and ripped a portal into existence. It smelled like the mortal realm, all dirt.

The young Skullstalker grumbled. But he bowed his head.

"Thank you for your time, brother," he muttered. Then he stepped through the portal, his fluffy tail dragging forlornly on the ground as he vanished through the portal.

Slate closed the portal and sighed, turning to Vale. "You are a much more welcome sight. Hello."

Vale stepped closer, cautious. Slate had never been so enthused to see his brothers until a few centuries ago, when his wife showed up.

"What did the whelp want?" Vale asked.

Slate laughed, and the noise sounded like rocks scraping together. "A wife."

"A wife?"

"Or a husband," Slate said. "He is not picky."

Vale frowned. "Are you providing them?"

"No. But I have a wife, as does our brother Wick."

Vale nodded. He had not met Wick before, but he had heard of their brother, who managed to undo the blood frenzy that had been with him since birth. Vale was glad for him. A blood frenzy sounded like it would get in the way of his work.

"But no," Slate continued. "I am not 'providing' wives *or*

husbands. If he wants one, he can find one himself. Speaking of wives... what brings you here?"

Vale growled. He did not like what Slate was implying. The mortal was not his *wife*. She was barely even an assistant. And she was—as she said—more trouble than she was worth. If he were not so desperate for assistance, he would have given her back to her lying mortals as soon as she got herself sprayed by that heatbloom.

If she got herself *sprayed*, he reminded himself. He had a sneaking suspicion that the void had gone out of its way to do so.

"Vale," Slate repeated. "What brings you here?"

Vale gnashed his fangs. "I told you it was impossible for a mortal to connect with my void."

"You did," Slate said. "Have you changed your mind?"

Vale's tail lashed. He was so used to being alone nowadays, he did not control his reactions. He would have to stop now that the mortal had arrived. Then again, he so rarely had reactions. His existence had narrowed down to one long day of work, with nothing worth reacting to.

"I think it used the pollen to open her up to it," Vale said reluctantly. "I think it *chose* her."

"You think? You are not certain?"

Vale thought back to the absolute lack of response he kept receiving whenever he asked his void a question. "I cannot commune with my void like I used to. I try, but it is muffled."

Slate hummed. He did not look overly concerned, but Slate

had never had as much communion with his void as Vale. Secretly, Vale thought it was because his older brother did not care for it as much as Vale did. The wilderness void required constant effort. Not like the wanderer's void, which looked almost identical whether Slate slept through the centuries or guided his wanderers out. Until his wife appeared, at least. She brought changes that Vale did not think were possible.

"You have been too busy since the light-motes died," Slate said. "You have lost the joy. As I lost it once. Perhaps this is your void's way of helping you find it again."

Vale stared at him, baffled. Surely, he could not be suggesting what Vale thought he was suggesting.

"Helping me find my *joy*," Vale repeated, waiting for Slate to correct him. "Through the *mortal*?"

Slate did not correct him. He only focused on something behind him, his lips spreading in a deep smile that could only mean one thing.

"Brother-in-law," cried Ruby as she came up behind Vale, tweaking his tail as she passed by him and wrapped her arm around her husband's waist. "How's your mortal? Have you visited Anderfel yet?"

"No," Vale snapped, taken aback by the tail-tweaking. Before the mortal, he had barely touched anyone in centuries. He cleared his throat, attempting to rein himself in. "You are sure our Anderfel brother would not know how to cure my void? If he is as adept at magic as you say, he could have some advice."

"I do not think he knows much about voids," said Slate

thoughtfully. "Then again, he is a mystery to me. Anytime I try to ask about his past, I am rebuffed."

"But he *can* help with the size problem," Ruby added unnecessarily, as if Vale had already forgotten about their prior conversation.

Then again, Vale had not encountered the size problem during their prior conversation. He shifted uncomfortably, his head full of memories—of how tight she had felt around him. How he had not been able to fit even half of his cock inside. How fervently she had begged for more, even when it was impossible. There was a good chance the pollen had not worked free of her blood, especially if the void had a say in it. He would probably be called upon to help her through it again.

"I will think about it," Vale said grudgingly.

Ruby beamed, her hair glowing with god-light. "And he can extend her lifespan!"

Vale snorted. That would be a serious binding ritual, tying the two of them together for eternity. He would not do that lightly.

"If she proves to be a helpful assistant, I will consider it," Vale said.

Weariness washed over him then, so powerful he staggered.

Slate caught him, his claws retracting as he dug his fingers into Vale's thick skin. "Brother?"

"It is nothing." Vale shook him off, straightening his robes. "My void weakens. I will fix it."

"This isn't just your void," Ruby said, her eyes flashing white. "When was the last time you rested?"

Vale could not answer. He rubbed his skull mask, the bone smooth and comforting against his claws.

"Go home," Slate said. "Sleep. You will feel better when you wake."

"But—"

Slate spoke over him. "It will not cure your void. But you must keep yourself well so you can do that yourself."

Vale held back an insolent remark. He used to think Slate was difficult to talk to when he slept the centuries away and snapped at Vale for waking him up. But somehow this relaxed, contented version of his older brother was more irritating.

"Thank you," Vale said, not feeling thankful in the least. "You have given me much to think about. I will go now."

He closed his eyes and focused on his void. As it pulled him back into the silver pool, he heard Ruby call after him:

"Do let us know how everything goes!"

Vale emerged from the silver pool in the wilderness void, annoyed and exhausted. They were treating this like an amusing story. His void was *sick*. If it got much worse, it would die, and Vale would die with it. *Then* where would they get the stories they found so entertaining?

Vale climbed out of the silver pool, his robes bone-dry. The crack embedded next to the pool had, predictably, gotten worse. Not much worse, only a small fracture bleeding out from the others. If he placed his clawed foot on top of it, the cracks were barely visible.

He frowned. He *was* too tired for such a small amount of damage. Maybe it would do him good to rest.

To his shock, a familiar, beloved voice echoed through his head.

Rest, it whispered.

Vale stilled. Part of him wanted to snarl at the voice: all these centuries of silence, and it showed up now, to tell him the very thing he *couldn't* do for so long?

"There is work to do," Vale argued, tail lashing angrily. "You are not well."

The void washed through him again. It was tired, just like him. But also, fond. So fond he almost choked on it. He had been working thanklessly for so *long*.

"Fine," Vale gritted. "But not for long. I have an assistant now; I will put her to work."

Another pulse ran through him. This one was joyful—perhaps the same joy Ivy had described earlier. The first thing it had shown her after she was sprayed with the heatbloom pollen.

Vale started toward his nest. The trees did not bend for him, and he sighed.

He understood his void less now than he ever did. But that did not matter now. He had a new duty: rest for a *very* short amount of time and then finally teach his mortal how to trim the eastern rib-thickets.

He arrived at his nest and stopped, spellbound.

He had expected to find it empty. To come across his troublesome new mortal locked in some other mishap. But Ivy was curled up in his nest, her red hair fanned out over the fur. Every time she breathed, the nest fell and rose with her breath.

Like she is part of my void, Vale thought dizzily. *Part of me.*

Long-dead emotions swelled inside him. He ignored it and climbed into the nest, angling himself awkwardly so as not to jostle her. He fell asleep easily, her warm scent dragging him into sleep's sweet embrace faster than ever before.

Eight

Two weeks later, Ivy dropped a rib-bone into a pile and stepped back with a triumphant smile.

"Done," she declared. She looked around the newly cleared eastern rib-thickets, but Vale was nowhere to be seen. Taking away another armful of excess bones, Ivy assumed. Once the bones had been stripped from the trees they were strangling, Vale took them to the nightbeast lair. Apparently, the nightbeasts used them as nests. The bones were also used for Vale's tool-crafting or, occasionally, crushed up for spell fodder.

Nothing in the void was wasted. Everything thrived off each other. Ivy loved watching it work, and she especially loved it when Vale explained things to her. His explanations were usually short and impatient, but sometimes he seemed to enjoy her questions rather than get annoyed by them, which was nice.

Ivy hated being an annoyance. She hoped she had been less of one since that disastrous first day in the wilderness void.

"Master Skullstalker," she called into the trees. "We're finished! Should we weed the teeth-lilies next? Or untangle the skull-saplings?"

No reply. Ivy craned her head, watching for a flash of antlers. When that didn't work, she hesitantly reached toward the void in her head.

The void immediately pulsed back at her. It felt happy enough. Tired, but that was normal. It felt more tired with each day that passed. The crack that started next to the silver pool portal was bigger now, reaching trees and bushes and sapping the darkness out of them. Everything that surrounded the silver pool had gone white. Ivy had never realized how intimidating that color could be until she saw all the poisoned plants around the pool.

Ivy looked around the dark forest, its bright bones and leaping corpsefrogs. It was horrifying, yes. But it was also alive, in its own strange way. How could she possibly be the one to kill it? To steal its keeper?

Vale emerged through the trees, stopping Ivy's thoughts in their tracks.

"Master!" Ivy beamed, waving like an idiot until she caught herself and stopped. "We're finished! Isn't it great?"

She spread her arms to display the trees ahead, which were mercifully un-strangled by wayward ribcages.

Vale barely glanced at them before stooping to gather the last pile of bones Ivy had plucked from the trees. He betrayed none of his tiredness, which Ivy knew he felt. The void let it creep into her sometimes: every day it got worse. Slowly, with Vale sleeping regularly, but still worse.

"Come," Vale said.

Ivy followed him, hiding her disappointment. And then, of course, her discomfort.

Vale glanced back at her. "Are you well?"

"Yes," Ivy said hastily.

"You are limping."

"Well, yes. That happens when..." Ivy flushed as she remembered the past two weeks, every day the pollen making itself known. And every day, he helped her through it.

Thoroughly. *Roughly*. Each time, she was afraid it would be the last. If she wouldn't literally die without it, would he still want to have her? She didn't want to find out. But she would have to. Even if the pollen didn't wear off before their month together was up, her Circle was still coming.

"I can just use my tongue," Vale offered. "I could ignore your begging."

Ivy giggled awkwardly as she remembered her fevered pleas. When the pollen came over her, she would say almost anything. Like how much she craved his big, inhuman cock and wouldn't have anything less.

"Do you..." Ivy avoided his eyes, watching a branch bend out of her way instead. "Do you *want* to ignore it?"

Vale didn't speak for several heart-stopping seconds. Long enough for Ivy's mind to race to every time that he touched her softly: pushing her hair out of her eyes with one gentle claw, shielding her face from the waterfall as he cleaned her after.

"It does not matter what I want," Vale said finally. "If you are too sore to work, you are useless to me."

It was a blow. But it was nothing Ivy hadn't heard before. It was why she had agreed to be the Skullstalker's offering in the first place: to be useful. Her uncle did love her, of that she had no doubt. But if she wasn't useful—gathering food, darning socks, and helping with the never-ending chores that came with constant travel—he would have left her at an orphanage when she was small.

"I'm not injured," Ivy insisted, flushing harder as she thought back to how Vale had examined her yesterday, prying her hole gently open to check for blood. "I'm just... tender."

The next step made pain radiate all the way up to her core. She winced again, and Vale stopped walking. Ivy started to protest, scared he would order her back to the nest again, but Vale only knelt on the forest floor.

Ivy frowned, unsure what to do. His arms were full of ribcages they picked from the thickets.

"Climb on my shoulder," Vale explained.

Ivy hesitated. Should she just... hop on? She'd never climbed on someone's shoulder before. Not even when she was a child and liable to be carried around. Besides, he grew weaker every day, even though he tried to hide it.

"Ivy," Vale prompted.

"You're tired," she said. "I shouldn't—"

Vale growled, more annoyance than threat. "Just do it."

Ivy sighed and heaved herself onto his robed shoulder, her legs dangling over his chest. Before she could settle, he stood up so fast she shrieked.

"Sorry," she said, clinging to his antlers.

She expected him to growl at her. Or brush her hands off his antlers, which she would let go of if she weren't so high up in the air. He was always startled when she touched them.

But Vale simply kept walking, his glowing green eyes fixed on the shrubbery as it peeled back to let them pass.

"I will fix this," Vale said. "There will be no more pain soon."

Ivy paled. Was he going to *eat* her? She thought they were getting along!

"What do you mean?" she stammered.

"There is a spell," he began, and she sagged against him with relief. "I would have gotten it sooner, but..."

He glanced down at the bones in his arms with an unreadable expression, his gait faltering. Then he looked up and his stride went back to normal—fast and focused, always heading to the next task.

"You are hurting," he continued. "I cannot have you distracted. I will do it today."

"Oh," Ivy said quietly. "Thank you."

Part of her was disappointed. She liked the pain, in an odd sort of way. It added to the pleasure of it all, like adding spice to her dinner.

She swayed with his steps, unable to shake the feeling that she should say more to thank him. But she knew he wouldn't appreciate it: whenever she let her touch linger, he pulled away. Sometimes there was a strange look on his face before he did so, or his eyes stayed on her for a long moment. But he always pulled away.

But she couldn't help it. She squeezed his antler, mostly because she wasn't sure he could even feel it. If he did, he didn't let her know. But his tail started to swish.

"The pollen," he said as they started coming close to the nightbeast territory, which was marked by significantly fewer trees and a giant skull that they resided inside. "How is it?"

"It's quiet today," Ivy said. "Maybe it finally left my blood."

Vale grunted. He stopped at the edge of the nightbeast territory. The giant skull where the nightbeasts resided sat in the middle of the suddenly sparse trees, stretching high above the tree line. It was so massive that Ivy hadn't even realized it was a skull at first. When she first asked what the skull was from, Vale had mentioned a "Titan." Ivy had never heard of them before, and Vale hadn't explained.

Vale emptied his armful of ribcages into the nightbeast territory. As soon as they clattered onto the forest floor, a long, cat-like creature poked out of the giant skull's eyeholes. Then another. One eyehole could fit at least a dozen of the huge beasts, which looked like they could take Ivy's head off with one clean swipe.

Ivy held back a gasp as the nightbeasts headed for the ribcages. They looked almost identical to the panthers she had seen in illustrations, except their black fur and skin were transparent. If the daylight caught them right, she could see all their muscles moving under their skin and their blood moving through their veins. Then they shifted out of the light, and they were solid once more.

"They're beautiful," Ivy whispered. "Should we leave?"

As soon as she asked, she realized it was a ridiculous question. No animal would attack a Skullstalker. Especially not when they were connected to his void.

The nightbeasts ignored them. They stalked up and started gnawing on the ribcages, their strong fangs crunching into them easily and licking at the marrow. Some of them—the older ones, Ivy noticed, with stiff joints and scarred fur—kept looking around expectantly. Not for other predators, Ivy realized. They looked almost... hopeful?

Ivy tugged on Vale's antler. "What are they looking for?"

Vale took a moment to reply. "The light-motes. They used to play with the beasts."

"Light-motes," Ivy repeated. "You mentioned them before. Your last assistants, right? A long time ago."

"Centuries," Vale said, watching the nightbeasts feast with distant eyes, as if he was remembering. "We thought it was a mistake when the first one died. Then they all started to dim. We never knew why. I asked for more, but the void never gave me any."

"The void *gave* them to you?"

"Yes," Vale said simply. "When I was chosen to come here, the void was overgrown. As it is now. The work was insurmountable. So, I asked for help. The void gave me the light-motes."

Chosen to come here, Ivy thought. She had never heard about Skullstalkers being chosen before. Was he chosen like *she* had been chosen? The idea made her shiver. Just because the void was in her head, that didn't mean she was eternally tied to it, right? Once her Circle came for her—came for *him*—the bond would sever and she would go back to her normal self.

Right?

Vale turned so abruptly that Ivy yelped, clinging to his antlers once again. He strode back through the trees, one clawed hand coming up to grip her thigh. Steadying her, she realized with a rush of strange glee.

"You smell afraid," he said. "There is no need to fear the nightbeasts. Like I said, nothing in this void will harm you."

"I'm not afraid of them." Ivy twisted to watch the night-beasts vanish in the trees as the path closed up behind them. "I mean it. They're beautiful."

Vale grunted again. His tail lashed, and Ivy wondered if he was lost in thought. His tail often moved when he was trying not to say something.

He had not let go of her leg. Ivy held her breath as they walked, relishing the feeling of his sharp claws twisting in the fabric of her shockingly clean dress.

"We will weed the teeth-lilies next," Vale said suddenly. "Then untangle the skull-saplings. Then tidy the bog. And we should ideally clean the castle—"

Ivy sat up, startled. "Castle?"

"Yes."

"You have a *castle*? Why?"

"It was here when I arrived," Vale replied. "There is only so much we can do. It crumbles more with each decade."

Ivy thought back to the castle she had spent her younger years in. The wide halls and gleaming marble floors, the lush carpets that were still not as lush as the fur lining Vale's nest.

"I grew up in a castle," she admitted quietly.

Vale hummed. "Were you important? Mortals consider castles important, yes?"

"Yes." Ivy grinned, all too pleased that he was asking her about herself. He had done so several times, but he usually cut himself off before he got too far. "But no, not because I was important. My uncle was important. He was the Royal Mage, assistant to the king. But he did not want to hurt his citizens like the king ordered, so they banished him. Now we gather allies to one day march on the castle, overthrow the king, and take our rightful place at the castle."

"And your uncle will be the leader of mortals," Vale said.

"All mortals in *this* country, yes," Ivy said. "Then I suppose I will be important. But it isn't about that. Honestly, I dread the day when people might pay attention to me. Whenever people pay attention, it's usually for a bad reason."

Vale said nothing for several seconds. Branches and bushes leaned out of their way, and Ivy reached to brush a branch above her head. It dipped down and touched her scalp, making her giggle in delight.

"Do you get yourself in trouble back in the mortal realm?" Vale asked.

Ivy sighed, resting her chin on his antlers. "I try not to. But

I keep making mistakes. Many of them are because I'm too busy admiring or reading about local fauna to notice the pot is burning, or that we've passed a crucial turn on the map. I guess that same thing happened with the heatbloom pollen. But at least it's helpful for being your assistant!"

She looked down at him, smiling hopefully. Vale wasn't looking at her, but his grip tightened on her thigh.

It made a telltale pulse of heat run through Ivy's core. She ignored it, clearing her throat. The pollen wasn't out of her blood yet, but that didn't mean they couldn't get some work done on the teeth-lilies first.

"You should tell me about yourself," she tried, letting her bare foot bounce against his chest. "I know hardly anything about you, and we're spending all this time together."

"There is nothing to tell," Vale replied. "I care for the void."

"But what do you *like* to do?" Ivy asked, her voice annoyingly high. Her skin was already heating up, her breath getting heavy. It was coming on surprisingly fast. It had been slower these past few days, giving her more warning before it rose up to engulf her.

"I told you," Vale said. "I am always working."

"I know. But what do you *like*?"

"It does not matter what I like," Vale said, eerily similar to something he had said to her earlier.

The rocking motion of his walk was making the pollen situation worse. Ivy crossed her legs, hoping he wouldn't smell it. Of course, he would eventually, but she still had time.

"What did you do before?" she tried, trying not to focus on

his clawed hand holding her leg. "When the light-motes were here, and you didn't have to work all the time?"

At first, Vale said nothing. But his tail lashed behind him. Ivy wanted it wrapped around her wrist. Or her throat. Wait, what?

Ivy held back a groan as she noticed how hot she was getting. Her face was hot, and she could feel herself getting wet. Why did this have to happen when she was finally getting him to open up?

"I liked to hunt," Vale admitted. "And commune with the plants instead of simply tending to them. I would have visitors. Sprites, nymphs, brothers. Sometimes we would go on... my brother Slate called them *adventures*."

"That sounds really nice," Ivy whispered. And it was *really* nice. Any other time, she would have been deeply charmed. But right now, all she wanted was for him to pin her to a tree and force that big cock into her.

Vale tilted his head. Ivy squeezed her legs together, heart pounding, waiting for him to notice.

But Vale only said, "Tell me of your people."

Ivy laughed hoarsely. "My... my people? The ones you think poisoned your void?"

"Yes. Them. Are they good to you?"

Ivy's smile faded. "What? Of course they are. Everyone's... great."

"You have many friends, then."

Ivy didn't reply. She had always felt like an outsider in the Circle, which shunned her for her constant mistakes. She sometimes made friends when they stayed in towns, but that happened less often now. Her uncle always warned her away from people outside the Circle, but she just couldn't help it. It was hard to stick to a group when they didn't want to hear what you had to say.

They're good people, she wanted to say. But she couldn't say that to Vale. Not when they were getting ready to chain him as they spoke.

"Um," Ivy whispered. "I guess? Everyone's— Yes, everyone's... great..."

She trailed off, her sore hole throbbing. The pollen raced through her body, lighting her up inside. She wanted his tongue again. She wanted his strange, flat-headed cock. She wanted the come that flooded out of it, always so much more than she could handle.

Ivy shifted uncomfortably. She was dripping into her dress. She could feel it pooling down her thighs. He had to smell it. She was right next to his face; there was no way he couldn't.

Vale took his hand off her leg. Ivy bit back a moan, clutching his antlers so tightly her hands ached almost as much as her cunt.

"You are dripping on me," Vale said.

"Sorry," Ivy gasped. But her hips were working, tiny thrusts she couldn't control as the pollen took over.

Vale plucked her off his shoulder and pressed her into a tree. The bone-bark was smooth and cool, just like him, and Ivy writhed against it.

"You did not say anything," Vale said, his green eyes flickering as he stared at her. "*Again*. Why?"

"I knew you w-would smell it," Ivy said weakly. She squirmed against his grip, gasping when his grip tightened around her waist. But still, he didn't reach for his robes. He just stood there, watching her squirm.

"Master Skullstalker," Ivy whined. She sounded pathetic and needy, but she couldn't stop it. "Mate me. *Please*."

Vale's tail lashed wildly. He leaned down, and Ivy's heart slammed in her chest as she thought he might kiss her. He had come close, she was sure of it, but he'd never closed the gap.

But before he could touch those strange pale lips to hers, the ground shook.

Ivy's mind lit up with panic. Not her own, she realized blindly as her vision whited out and her mind filled with borrowed emotion, too big for her head to handle. She cried out, grabbing her head as the panic slowly retreated, only a headache to prove it had been there at all.

Vale was frozen. He still had her pinned to the tree, but as soon as Ivy became aware of him again, he lowered her down so fast she stumbled.

"What *was* that?" Ivy gasped, tears streaming down her face.

"The void," Vale replied. His glowing eyes were closed, his voice strained. Like it had pained him, too. "Stay there."

"No! I can help!" Ivy protested, wiping wildly at her face. She managed one step before falling to the ground, the pollen surging through her so hard it made her cry out.

Vale stumbled along with her. Despite all his attempts to hide it, he got worse along with the void. He took a hesitant, jerky step toward her. Then he stopped, and she imagined her wet scent filling his lungs. How pitiful she must have looked.

But Vale had bigger things to worry about than a pollen-stricken assistant. He turned and fled, following the void to where it was hurting.

Ivy fell to the ground, panting, trying to stop herself from reaching between her sore legs. She wanted to help Vale, to be *useful* for once. But even with the void's panic still fading from her mind, the pollen couldn't be denied. It was coiling, threatening to burn her up if Vale didn't come back.

And soon.

Nine

The silver pool was turning milky white.

"There is nothing I can do," Vale told it, scratching uselessly at the pale cracks spreading through the ground that surrounded the pool. "Why did you call me here if I could do nothing? Why strike my mortal down with a pollen-frenzy and then pull me away? What are you *doing*?"

There was no answer. Vale roared, furious and more worried than he had been in millennia.

"I should be hunting down those mortals!" he snarled, straightening and shaking dirt off his claws. "Or—or a spell! Anything to cure you! Yet, you insist I spend my days with the usual errands. If I do not find a way to cure you, you will die. We will *both* die! Is this panic, this *shaking*— Is this you only realizing this now, after it bleeds into your precious pool? Just tell me where to go, and I will go!"

He closed his eyes, listening hard.

Weak wind through the trees. Distant root-deer hooves. Ivy's whimpers, full of pain and need.

Finally, the void gave him the smallest whisper: *go to her.*

Vale laughed, sharp and rumbling. "And *then* what? How is she helping? She has only made things *worse*!"

The void trickled a thin river of disappointment through him. Vale did not have to ask why.

Go to her, it whispered again, so quiet that Vale could hardly hear it over the wind.

Vale ignored it. He took a step toward the pool, intent on finding Ivy's mortals and demanding answers. They had to be the cause of this. They *had* to.

But another one of Ivy's desperate moans drifted through the trees. The branches even parted to show him the way, shuddering with effort.

Vale glared at the tiny cracks surrounding the pool. At the white spots bleeding into it, threatening to spread its rot into every crevice of the void. He needed to fix this. But if he lost his only assistant— If he lost *Ivy*, his only visitor in centuries, who smiled at nightbeasts and giggled at the vines that stroked her cheek and worked almost as hard as he did—

Vale growled and turned, stomping down the path the void had made for him. He would take care of his assistant. Then he would abandon his needless bone thicket clearing and teeth-lily weeding and find a way to fix his damn void.

. . .

Ivy was slumped against the ground when he returned. She had tried crawling after him, he realized. She truly did want to help, even if she was stricken by an illness the void had forced upon her.

Ivy stared up at him, her eyes wet. Her hips worked against the ground, but she ignored them.

"The... void," she said, her voice thick. "I felt it. It's in pain."

"It is no more hurt than usual," Vale lied. He bent down, letting her hot, sweet scent wash over him. "But *you* are in incredible pain."

Ivy pushed herself up on trembling elbows. "I can... If you need to go, I can..."

Vale could hear the need in her voice. If he left, she would only worsen. And if he was honest with himself—which he had been, lately, to a worrying degree—Vale did not want to leave. He was too busy to consider what he wanted these days. But thanks to her infuriating presence, he knew enough of himself to realize that he wanted his assistant almost as much as she wanted him.

Vale picked her up and straightened, shoving her against the same tree he had pinned her against before, watching her gasp and writhe as her legs dangled high off the ground. Then he ran a claw down her gauzy dress, ripping it down the middle until it fell off her in halves.

Ivy moaned, grinding against him even as her face contorted in worry. "My dress!"

"The void will fix it," Vale growled. "The void poured all of itself into you, even though it sickens every day. You strange, *frustrating* little gift."

He hoisted her up the tree and wound his long tongue around her breasts, laving them until they were dripping.

"So confoundingly *soft*," Vale continued. "Every time, I have to hold myself back from sinking my teeth in."

He pressed his fangs around her left nipple. Then he let the pressure build until a bead of blood welled on the underside.

Ivy's chest heaved under his touch, gorgeous moans dripping out of her as heavily as the slick between her legs.

Vale licked up the small drop of blood, imagining he could taste the pollen. He felt crazed with her scent, even before he had tasted her. Her sweet, delicious heat and the small, sour fear buried underneath.

Despite the fear, Ivy canted her hips against him. "More! Please, more."

"It will hurt," Vale warned.

"The pollen is already hurting me," Ivy gasped. "At least give me the hurt I *want*."

Vale rubbed his lips against her neck, feeling the blood pulse underneath her overheated skin. He could use his tongue. But he did not know if he had the willpower to deny her like he had that first time. Even smelling the pain drifting between her legs, her tiny hole aching after days of satisfying her pollen-lust, was not enough to deter him.

Not when she whined for it like that.

"There is a spell," he told her again. "I can go to the mortal realm. I have a brother in Anderfel—"

"No!" Ivy grabbed his antlers, her eyes puffy with needy tears. "Vale, don't go. Take me right here. Please, I need it."

Vale stared at her, bowled over with the force of his desire that washed over him as he said his given name instead of that confounding title that she had given him. He had spent so long convinced that he no longer wanted anything, surviving on so little food and sleep and company that if the light-motes were around, they would have worried for him. But here was the evidence pumping through him, as undeniable as his own heartbeat: he wanted. He wanted Ivy so badly, his mouth watered with it.

"Say it again," he demanded.

Ivy spoke instantly. "Please."

He shook his head, feeling her small hands flex around his antlers. "No. My name. Say it."

"Vale," she gasped.

He growled helplessly and took his cock out of his robes, letting a thick river of spit drip from his tongue to his cock before lining himself up to Ivy's entrance and pressing inside.

Ivy wailed. She was crying; he could smell the salt even if he wasn't staring at her red, puffy face. But he could also smell her desire, hot and dripping as he fucked her as shallowly as he could manage.

He pinned her against the tree, mating her with no more than his cockhead. The stretch was still immense; he could feel her strain to her limits every time he pressed in. But he didn't push further, no matter how much he wanted to. He had seen her wince through her pleasure every time he hit the end of her hole. And even when he filled her fit to bursting, he could never get as deep as they both wanted.

Vale would go to the mortal realm to find his brother as soon as the pollen subsided. It was not so much a decision as much as it was a calling, cursing himself for waiting this long. He had gotten so distracted with his duties. *She* was his duty now, as much as the rib-thickets and the teeth-lilies. His sweet, determined little gift, who needed his cock so badly that she would die without it.

"More," Ivy moaned, tears slipping down her plump cheeks. "Vale, please, *more*."

Vale licked her tears. He ran his clawed hands over her breasts, the soft folds of her stomach, her plump thighs. Would she beg for him like this after the pollen finally ran its course? Would they even have time to find out, with the void decaying around them and Vale getting weaker along with it?

His legs shook. Ivy was not heavy, despite her insistence that she was heavier than many humans. But the weariness kept creeping into him, even with him sleeping more often than ever before.

"Please," Ivy whimpered. "Please, *please*."

Vale could take it no longer. He shoved inside as deep as he could and came with a roar. Ivy cried out, first in shock and then in ecstasy as her own release washed over her. Her hole squeezed deliciously around his pulsing cock, her fluids joining his as they dripped down her legs.

They stayed there like that, breathing in tandem. Ivy touched the moss on his skull mask, and Vale pulled back to see her expression.

There was no disgust in it. There never was. Just curiosity and that odd wonder he had never seen on a mortal before her.

Vale pulled out with a slick noise as his come emptied out of her. Ivy flushed, as she always did when the pollen subsided.

"I'm alright," she insisted as Vale knelt to check her hole. She kept gripping his antlers, as if he would ever let her fall.

Vale growled weakly, ignoring her protests. She smelled of pain, the sour scent growing larger underneath the fading pleasure.

"I am," Ivy said. "I'm—*oh*!"

Vale ran his tongue up her legs, cleaning up their combined mess. Ivy spread her legs obligingly, and Vale relished the tremble in them as he licked his spend from her hole.

There was no blood mixed in. This was good. Vale gave her one last thorough lick and then stood, lapping up the small drop of blood he had bit into her breast. The urge to bite down intensified, but he ignored it. He had no blood-frenzy. This was one want he would happily ignore.

He stooped to pick up Ivy's dress. It was whole, as he had predicted. He lifted Ivy into his arms and dropped the dress on top of her, watching her slide her hands over it in surprise.

"I told you," he said. "My void likes you."

It did not make him feel as bitter as it often did. He could not fault his void for liking Ivy. He liked her, too. More than he was comfortable with.

Vale started through the forest, where a path was being cleared for them.

"Where are we going now?" Ivy whispered, holding her dress over her front.

"You are going to my nest," he replied. "I must go to visit my brother in Anderfel."

Ivy's eyes widened. "For the spell that will... make me have no pain?"

"You need not worry," he assured her.

They arrived at his nest. Vale placed her in the center, watching her slick, flushed body squirm against the furs. What was he supposed to do with all this *want*? He had never craved like this; he was sure of it. Maybe that was another reason why he had been delaying this spell: with nothing to hold him back, his desire could grow even more.

He did not want it to. He had duties to perform and a void to save. He did not have time to rut a mortal senseless, especially when her pollen-sickness was fading.

Vale straightened, adjusting his robes over his spent cock.

"I will be back soon," he promised.

His Anderfel brother's home was... strange.

It was dark, like he expected. But this darkness was nothing he had seen in the mortal realm. This felt like a void, even though he was sure he had stepped into the mortal realm when he used the silver pool. Had it sent him to the wrong place?

There was a speck of light in the distance. Vale stepped

toward it, the darkness so thick it clung to his robes as he walked. The shadows stunk of sulfur, and Vale growled in displeasure.

"Oh, good," came a quiet, raspy voice from the light ahead. "I thought it was the small one again, come to beg for a companion."

"Who?" Vale asked, unable to stop himself.

"The small one," the voice repeated. "With purple eyes. He lives not far from here. He keeps coming to ask me to help him get a wife."

"A wife," Vale repeated, a memory stirring in his head: a young Skullstalker kneeling in front of Slate, sounding dejected as Slate declined him.

"Or a husband," the voice continued. "He is not fussy. Come closer. My eyes are not what they were."

Vale approached slowly, squinting into the light. After another few steps, a figure became clear.

The Skullstalker was old. So old it confused Vale, who had always thought that Slate was the oldest of them all. This creature's skin sagged, and his skull mask was chipped with age. Instead of glowing, his eyes were grey and cloudy. The old Skullstalker bared his teeth, showing several missing fangs. It took Vale a moment to realize he was not being threatened; this was a smile.

"You are new," the Skullstalker said happily. "It is good to meet you."

"You as well," said Vale cautiously. "My brothers insist you can help me."

The Skullstalker shrugged, such an odd movement from a Skullstalker that it shocked Vale into silence.

"I will do my best," said the Skullstalker humbly. "Come, come. Tell me your woes."

He turned. Vale followed him, his claws fully extended. Slate had assured Vale he could trust this stranger, but how could he when even Slate did not know his name after all this time?

A cave appeared through the shadows, huge and looming. The Skullstalker hobbled calmly into it, then turned back to face him.

"You came here because you need something," said the Skullstalker. "That is the only reason any soul visits me. That, or to tell me what has become of them after I sent them away the first time."

"What has become of them?"

The Skullstalker smiled again. "It is the one thing I require. If I help you, you must come back and tell me what happened because of my assistance. I am attached to my cave, but I get so little entertainment here."

Vale eyed him warily. This was perhaps the strangest Skullstalker he had ever met. Then again, he had not met many. They were a solitary species.

"So," the Skullstalker continued. "What would you wish of me? Let me guess... your size has become a problem with your mortal paramour?"

"One of many," Vale said. "But not the most pressing."

"Oh?" The Skullstalker's cloudy eyes glinted. "Well. Let us get that taken care of, and then we can move on."

He limped over to the wall of the cave and lifted a jar of black oil off a shelf.

"What must be done?" Vale asked.

The Skullstalker shushed him, dipping a clawed finger into the black oil and reaching for Vale's face.

Vale jerked back instinctually with a snarl.

"I only mean to help," the Skullstalker assured him. He raised his dripping claw again.

Vale forced himself to calm. Even tired as he was, he could still rip this old Skullstalker in two with little effort.

He stilled. The Skullstalker ran his wet claw over Vale's skull, tracing patterns that Vale did not understand. After a brief pause to run two dark slashes down his collarbones, he pricked his thumb. Then he pricked Vale's, dripping their combined blood into the jar of oil.

He dipped his claw back in and drew one drop on Vale's lower lip.

Vale eyed him distrustfully. "It is almost done?"

"Almost," the Skullstalker said.

With that, he bowed his head and started to chant.

Vale did not recognize the words. But unlike the symbols, these words awakened some strange awareness in him. Like something he had heard when he was very small.

His groin began to tingle. The tingle soon expanded, filling Vale until the tip of his tail vibrated with the spell. Then all at once it was over, leaving Vale shaking and gasping, curling over as his vision tunneled.

The Skullstalker patted his back. "There, there, little brother. You will find no more pesky size problems with your lover. Now, tell me about this other problem."

Vale braced himself against the cave wall. He did not like this strange Skullstalker touching him like they knew each other, though he forced himself to tolerate it. He was helping, after all.

Vale forced himself to straighten, his legs still trembling and his head spinning. "My void... it has been poisoned. Do you know how to fix it?"

The Skullstalker blinked, surprised. He reached a gaunt hand out to touch Vale's chest, and Vale gritted his fangs through an unwanted touch from someone he did not know. He would put up with much worse if it meant fixing his void.

"You have a deeper relationship with your void than any of our surviving brothers," the Skullstalker said, pulling his hand back. "What has your void told you?"

"It tells me nothing! It only urges me to continue my everyday duties, and insists—" Vale stopped, his mind full of images of his mortal offering.

"Insists?" the Skullstalker prompted.

"There is a mortal who... started it all. She did not mean to. But my void insists she can help."

"If she is the one who started it all," the Skullstalker began.

Vale growled, talking over him. "But she does not KNOW how she started it! Perhaps she can help. Or perhaps my void is lacking judgment! It is old. Older than me. It did not give me back my light-motes. It imprinted on a mortal the second she entered—"

"Then push her out."

Vale faltered. "What?"

"Remove her from your void," the Skullstalker explained, wiping black oil on the cave wall behind him. "If the void improves, then she is the problem."

Vale paused. He had the same thought, once. Of course, he had. But...

"The void would *tell* me if she was the problem," Vale said. "If she were the poison... If she were making us sick, then it would *force* her out."

"Would it?" the Skullstalker asked, hobbling over to the shelf and placing the jar of black oil in its place. "You do not sound like you trust its judgment."

Vale swallowed. He felt guilty in a way he had not felt since the light-motes died, somehow sure that it was his fault. That if he had worked harder, he could have saved them.

"The mortal has a good heart," he tried. "She is dedicated and hardworking, even if she gets into trouble. She would be good for the void, if it were not sick."

"I am not saying to banish her *forever*," the Skullstalker said, straightening the other jars on the black-splattered shelf. "Just put her out. If the void continues to sicken, you can do what you wish. But if the void improves... well, then. It would be good if you threw her out."

Vale said nothing. He had wished to banish her, not so long

ago. But not after these last weeks. Not after he had seen how hard she worked, how fascinated she was by the plants he used to love so much. Not after tasting her, filling her, curling around her in his nest. She looked at him with such surprise whenever he allowed himself to touch her gently. There was a part of him that he did not know existed, a part of him that wanted...

Vale forced the thought away and wiped the remaining black oil off his skull mask.

"Thank you," he said gruffly. "You have given me much to think about. I will take my leave."

He turned to leave, only stumbling once before righting himself and walking out of the cave.

The Skullstalker's quiet voice called after him through the dark. "Come back when it is finished. This sounds like a story I wish to hear more of."

Ivy was asleep when he returned.

Vale watched her chest rise and fall, his tail lashing mightily behind him. He would not get to test the Skullstalker's size spell after all. If this worked, Ivy's departure would fix everything.

This is what you must do, he told himself. *Do not hesitate.*

But he did not move. He noticed there were vines. Strange vines covered in dark leaves, twining up her legs and threading through her wild red hair.

Vale growled. "What is your obsession with this mortal? She must go. If it works, then you are cured. If it does not, I will bring her back. You can rot and die with your precious mortal inside you."

Ivy stirred. But she did not wake, too tired from their coupling earlier. She smelled sweaty and sore and satisfied, her scent filling Vale's nose like the sweetest temptation he had ever known.

He had never been tempted until she showed up. Maybe it would be better if she never came back.

The thought sent a river of pain through him. And something else.

You want her to stay, too, whispered the void.

Vale's claws pricked into his palms. "It does not matter what I want. I do what is best for you. For *both* of us."

He stood a moment longer, watching the leaves curl around Ivy's soft face. Then he leaned down.

Ten

Ivy awoke to a leaf brushing her cheek.

She fumbled at it, prying her eyes open. It was ivy, she realized with surprise. Her namesake plant. The same species of ivy that had climbed her castle walls when she was small. The same ivy that had sprung to life on the riverbank on her first day in the void.

Something loomed over her.

Ivy startled. Then she spotted Vale and laughed with relief.

"You scared me," she said. She shifted in the nest, holding back a wince as her body ached. "I thought there was no ivy in this void."

She expected him to tell her that he called it another name here. But Vale only looked down to where the ivy was climbing up his clawed foot. He was silent for so long that Ivy started to worry.

Then he said, "Is that what this is?"

"Yes." Ivy sat up, untangling a vine of ivy from her hair. "It's so strange. This is the same species of ivy that was on the castle when I lived there as a child. I haven't seen it in years."

The ivy was resistant. Ivy pulled harder, wincing as it came free from her messy hair. Then she gasped, a memory coming through her sleep-addled mind.

"You're back," she said. "You said you were going to get that spell. Did it... happen?"

She snuck a look at his robes. Everything looked the same, which could mean nothing. Magic was magic, after all. Looks were deceiving.

Vale didn't reply. The ivy vine tangled tighter in Ivy's hair, winding up her arm and squeezing.

"Hey!" Ivy laughed, pulling herself free. But not before she got a pulse from the void, timed perfectly with the ivy's squeezes as she tore it away. The void was sad. No, the void was *mourning*.

She looked up at Vale, panicked. "What's wrong?"

Vale said nothing. But his tail swished, his jaw clenched tight. Then, so fast Ivy hardly saw it, he bent down and scooped her up, walking into the trees.

"Wait," Ivy said. "What are you doing? Where are we going?"

Trees didn't bend out of their way like they usually did. Branches scraped against Vale's arms, and bushes were trampled under his feet. A leaf spiraled into Ivy's lap, and she brushed it away right as she recognized what it was: ivy. The ivy vines were racing over the trees above her, trying to follow them.

"You must leave," Vale said, staring straight ahead as he carried her toward the silver pool that would deliver her back to the mortal realm.

Ivy went cold. Had she been found out? She would almost be relieved if he weren't forcing her away. She had thought about telling him so many times, only to stop at the last second. She had known Vale for a mere two weeks; she couldn't betray her family for him.

"But—" Ivy tried.

"I am sorry," Vale said over her, his gait increasing. "I must fix this void."

"And making me leave will help how?"

"It may not. But I must try. If your very presence is the poison—"

It's not my presence, Ivy wanted to scream. *It was that stupid little vial my uncle got me to empty into the silver pool! I feel worse about it every day!*

"But the pollen sickness," Ivy stammered.

"There will be mortals to help you," Vale said. His tail swished so hard that it broke a nearby branch. "It is likely the void that is making *you* sick," Vale continued, sounding bitterly amused. "That seems like something it would do. Make the pollen stay in your blood, to keep bringing us together. To—to make us *attached* to each other."

Ivy shrank back at the venom in his voice. Then she spotted the silver pool through the trees and struggled up in his arms.

"Is that so bad?" Ivy demanded shakily. "I—I've been happy here. Happier than I thought I could ever be in a Skullstalker void! Let me stay, we can fix this together!"

Another ivy leaf fell around her face. A vine wrapped around Vale's antler, pulling him back before he yanked himself free and came to the edge of the silver pool.

"See?" Ivy yelled. "The void doesn't want me to go!"

Vale growled, gripping her arms and holding her up in front of his face. "You think you know my void better than *me*? We are eternally entwined! You are a visitor! You are a mortal and will die before the century is out!"

Ivy's eyes pricked with tears.

Vale growled louder, but his grip loosened. "If it worsens, there is no point in you being here. If it gets better once you are gone, then you should *stay* gone."

Before Ivy could protest, he carried her into the silver pool.

Shiny water rushed around Ivy's face. It was corroded with the smallest hint of sickly white, the scent so acrid it almost made Ivy gag.

Then they rose out of the water, into the mortal realm. They were standing in a dirt circle in front of the stone slab Ivy had been tied to when her uncle presented her as an offering. Her blood was still on the ground, tacky with age.

Ivy rubbed her arm where he had healed her cut. Then she yelped as Vale stomped over and set her down unceremoniously on the stone slab.

"What about our trade?" Ivy said. "You said you'd give us weapons!"

Vale snarled. "Our deal was forfeit when your people *poisoned* my void!"

"You don't know if that's what happened," Ivy tried, choking up with the betrayal of it all. Not because of what Vale was doing, but because of what *she* was doing, still. Lying to him after weeks of plucking bones from trees. Watching him painstakingly untangle a corpsefrog from a vine and send it on its way. He was rough and strange and otherworldly, but he was not a beast. And Ivy had doomed his void to death and him to a life of pain and servitude.

Vale turned back toward the dirt circle. Then he growled, turning back.

"This could be temporary," he said. "If my void continues to sicken—"

"Which it will," Ivy croaked, kneeling up on the stone slab. "Vale, I'm *not* the poison! The poison was—"

She stuttered to a stop. But it was too late. Vale stopped, his tail stilling and his glowing eyes fixing on her.

"Ivy?"

It wasn't a threat. Ivy might have preferred it if it were. But Vale's gravelly voice was full of betrayal, so thick it choked her.

Ivy wiped at her wet cheeks. "Th-the poison was..."

Vale's head snapped up.

Like a dog scenting a rabbit, Ivy thought, dazed.

She twisted on the stone slab, looking desperately around

the forest. Were the Circle back? They couldn't be. They had weeks before they were due back.

And yet...

Vale breathed in, catching their scent. His glowing green eyes narrowed at the dark woods ahead.

Ivy turned, heart in her throat. Something was glinting in the dark. She couldn't make it out from here, but she knew what it meant. It was the tell-tale glint of her uncle's crossbow, raised ready to fire.

"Wait," Ivy blurted.

She shot to her feet.

An arrow spun through the darkness.

Vale roared, moving for her. But while Skullstalkers were fast, an arrow was faster.

The bolt hit her just above her heart. Ivy stumbled back, raising a dazed hand to touch the arrow sticking into her. It was wrapped in malblossom, a flower she had helped them find when her uncle told her of his newest plot. It was the only mortal plant they knew of that could harm a Skullstalker.

Oh good, Ivy thought, dazed, as she rubbed the small white flowers that surrounded the arrow protruding from her skin. *That would have really hurt him.*

Vale roared. Her uncle yelled something back, but Ivy couldn't hear it over the blood rushing through her ears.

She crumpled toward the stone. A huge clawed hand caught her, and Ivy found her cheek pressed against Vale's cool collarbone. His fangs were bared, his green eyes glowing brighter than she'd ever seen them.

Another yell. This time, Ivy could hear it.

"*Fire*, damn you," her uncle screamed.

She looked up just in time to see a second arrow streaking out of the darkness, right toward Vale's head.

Eleven

Vale snatched the arrow out of the air and snapped it in two.

The malblossom twining wrapped around the weapon burned deep into his hand. He ignored it, cradling Ivy close as he watched the mortals pour out of the tree line.

There were six. Three men and three women, all bearing weapons except for one man who was holding two logs of firewood and looking scared out of his wits. One woman had half the straps of her breastplate on, the other straps hanging uselessly and making her breastplate clang against her chest.

They had not expected him, Vale realized as Christopher Silverpetal charged to the front of the group, swapping his crossbow for a mage's staff. None of his other arrows were tied with malblossom, only those first two. The second had been so clumsily adorned that most of the malblossom had fallen off mid-flight, scattering to the forest floor below.

"Skullstalker," called Christopher, pointing his mage's staff at him. That infuriating vial still dangled from it, swinging distractingly. "You-you startled us! We thought you were something else."

"Another Skullstalker, perhaps," Vale snarled. "Standing at the stone slab where you offered up your niece to me?"

"*Perhaps*," Christopher repeated, even mimicking Vale's raspy accent. "You cannot be too careful. You understand. Speaking of my niece, might I have her back? She looks... unwell."

"Because you *shot* her," Vale roared. "And *poisoned* my void!"

He crouched, ready to spring. The mortals raised their weapons again, including the man with the firewood, who held it protectively in front of him.

"Well, that didn't go quite as we hoped," Christopher said in a rush. He raised his staff, that irritating vial swinging with the motion.

Ivy stirred weakly in Vale's arms. Vale, who had never had anything to protect during a fight, looked down.

"NOW," Christopher screamed.

A deluge of arrows and spells flew at him. Vale dodged and broke arrows and knocked a sword out of a charging man's hand, sending him flying into the man carrying the firewood. Then he stomped on both men at once, blood splattering up his leg.

The women came for him next. He threw them all into a tree, which cracked under the force.

Christopher barked a hoarse laugh. "Hells! They did *not* exaggerate about your power, Skullstalker. You are every bit as deadly as they say!"

Vale yanked a useless, unadorned arrow out of his shoulder and growled. "You poisoned my void!"

"*She* poisoned your void," Christopher corrected with a sweaty grin. He danced backward, his staff trained on Vale's face.

Vale dodged the fire spell that Christopher had aimed, then lunged, grabbing Christopher by the throat. It would be so easy to snap his flimsy neck, but he held himself back. If he weren't so thirsty for blood, he would have yanked that infuriating vial off so it would stop swinging for once.

"FIX IT," he roared.

"I..." Christopher scrabbled at Vale's claws around his throat. For some insufferable reason, he was still grinning. Like this was all some adventure and not his last day on earth. "I can't! She'll tell you!"

Vale glanced down.

Ivy stared up at him, her plump face pale. For once, her blood was not a temptation.

Vale brushed her hair out of her face. "Does he tell the truth?"

Ivy's brow wrinkled. "I... I think so. He never said anything about an antidote."

"There is none," Christopher choked, still dangling from Vale's fist.

Vale grunted. Then he raised Christopher higher into the air, ready to crush his puny throat.

"Wait," Ivy croaked. "Don't kill him."

Vale did not take his eyes off Christopher's reddening face. He was still smiling, although it was slowly stopping as consciousness drained from him at the lack of oxygen.

Ivy touched Vale's chest. "He's my only family."

Vale entertained a vivid fantasy of crushing the mage's throat anyway. Then he dropped Christopher on the ground, letting the man wheeze and gasp.

Vale trod on his staff. It snapped, making Christopher cry out hoarsely.

"It does not matter how weak I am," Vale growled. "I will kill anyone who enters my void without my permission."

With that, he turned to leave.

"You cannot escape us," Christopher yelled hoarsely. "Soon you will be so weak you won't be able to do anything but bend to our will!"

"And then I will die with my void before you can take back your precious castle," Vale growled. "Outstanding work, mortal."

He stepped into the dirt circle. But before he could will them back to his void, Ivy spoke up again.

"Wait," she said, sitting up in his arms. It looked like a significant effort, her head wobbling before she straightened. "Let me talk to him. I can— I can talk him out of it."

She did not sound certain. But she *did* sound determined.

Vale looked at the blood staining her dress. He did not know how much blood mortals could lose. But she was still talking and moving, which meant he had time.

"I will let you *try*," he allowed.

He turned cautiously back to Christopher, who was still lying on the ground, massaging his throat and cradling the broken top of his staff, which still had the annoying vial attached to it.

Christopher snorted when he saw his niece staring at him. "So, you seduced the monster after all, hmm? You were always so dedicated to my cause."

"There are many things you can use for weapons in the void," Ivy said, her hand pressed just above where the arrow was inside her. "Just take them and go. You don't need to bind him."

Christopher sighed and rubbed a hand over his sweaty forehead. "Given that you collapsed from a single crossbow wound, I take it he hasn't made you a god."

"No."

"Do you have any powers?"

Ivy hesitated. Vale waited to see if she would tell him about the void and their impossible connection.

"No," Ivy said again.

Christopher nodded. He sat back against the forest dirt and twirled the front half of his snapped staff. The vial tied to it spun with it, and Vale ground his fangs together at its annoying glinting.

"Well," he said. "You've obviously chosen your side."

"I haven't," Ivy protested. "I'm your family! I just know that this isn't the way. Uncle, please listen."

"He does not seem very weak," Christopher said over her, raising his voice until it rang through the trees and using the front half of his broken staff to point at the corpses lying around their small battlefield.

"Did you even use all the poison?" Christopher continued.

Ivy wilted with shame. "I... did."

She looked up at Vale, who stared back at her impassively. He should have known. The void *did* know, but it did not tell him for some ridiculous reason. Though as soon as he thought of it, he knew the answer: It knew he would banish her, and it wanted her to stay.

Christopher hummed, drawing their attention back. "Can you tell us anything about it?"

Vale growled.

"No," Ivy said over him. "I'm sorry, Uncle. I think you should leave it be."

"*Do* you now?" Christopher laughed, slapping his knee like she had said something humorous. "Those Skullstalker plants must be something truly spectacular. Unless it's something *else* about the Skullstalker worth betraying your family for?"

"It's not about the plants," Ivy insisted. "The void is alive. It's alive, and it feels things. *He* feels things! He's not a beast. He's... he's good."

Ivy looked up at him again. Her eyes were wet, and she

stunk of pain so badly it made him ache. His anger at her deeds was already draining. She had done something terrible, but she was trying to make up for it. She was even risking death for it. Nobody had done something like that for Vale in a long time.

"And for him, you'd give up your duty to the Circle of the Jeweled Fist?" Christopher demanded. "Your duty to *me*?"

"No," Ivy whispered. "Of course not. I just won't let you..."

Her eyes rolled up in her head. She fell limp in Vale's grip, head lolling against his chest.

"Ivy?" Vale snapped.

"Shame she didn't get to finish," Christopher called, spinning the top half of his broken staff lazily. "But we can assume what she said, hmm? She won't let me take you. Let me guess, you let her eat the scraps after you were finished with your dinner?"

Vale ignored him, pressing his ear to her chest and listening. Her heartbeat was weak.

"I'll tell you," Christopher continued. "One nice deed, and that girl would do anything. I mean, *anything*! It was a real problem when she got to talking to folk outside of the Circle. But I guess I'll let you have her next. I'll charm her back, of course. After this mess is done with, I'll grovel and she'll—"

Vale roared so loudly that Christopher dropped his broken staff and clutched his ears. Vale took one hard step out of the circle, then stopped.

He had promised Ivy. Even if he had not, she was running out of time. He needed to stop the bleeding.

"If I ever see you again," Vale growled. "I *will* snap your neck. I do not care what she says."

Christopher said nothing. He was still groaning on the ground, his hands over his ears.

Vale stepped back into the circle and closed his eyes, holding Ivy so tightly to his chest he feared he might crush her.

He appeared safely in the silver pool. Ivy was still slumped in his arms, her breathing dangerously shallow.

He stumbled out of the pool. He did not check to see if anyone had followed; the void was not so weak as to allow someone in without its permission.

The forest parted to let Vale through. Leaves swayed toward Ivy as he ran, holding her steady.

He reached the nest and placed her inside. Then he turned to the tree that was drooping over him, offering something.

"Thank you," Vale said hoarsely as it dropped the soothepine into his palm. He crammed the leaves into his mouth, chewing hard. Then he took the arrow in Ivy's chest and braced himself.

It did not take much. Just a small yank, and the arrow slid from Ivy's chest with a slick *pop*. Ivy's reaction, however, was awful. Her eyes snapped open, her back bowing as she sobbed in agony.

Vale threw the bloody, malblossom-wrapped arrow into the forest, ignoring the burns it scored into his fingers. Then he spat into her wound. The green leaf-spit dripped into the arrow hole, burrowing through the blood and glowing as it slowly healed her wound.

Ivy whimpered. Vale stroked her hair, a concerned rumble in his throat.

"You will heal," he assured her. "We are here. All will be well."

Those leaf-vines from before—*ivy*, she had called it, her namesake from the mortal realm—snaked into the nest and curled around her limbs. Strands threaded gently through her hair, stroking along with Vale.

"We are here," Vale repeated quietly.

Ivy's eyelids fluttered. Her writhing stilled, the fight leaving her. But before Vale could panic that he was too late, Ivy's injury glowed brighter.

It was not the soothepine. Not *just* the soothpine, anyhow. That much was clear as the glow spread to her eyes, shining between her eyelashes.

I know that green, Vale thought. It was not the green of Ivy's own eyes. It was the green of *his*. The green of the wilderness void.

Ivy's mouth opened. Green light poured from it. Her skin glowed, green light radiating through her until her whole body shone.

Vale stared, spellbound. He had seen magic every day of his long existence. But he had not *felt* it like this, beautiful and blessed, for millennia.

Suddenly, Ivy sagged. Her eyes drooped shut, and her body went limp.

Vale climbed into the nest with her and pulled her into his lap. He did not understand what had just happened. But he knew one thing for certain:

Ivy was not going anywhere.

Twelve

Ivy was having an incredible dream.

She was lying in Vale's nest, cocooned in his arms. Plants swarmed over her, sending pulses of affection and safety through her skin. Her chest throbbed with discomfort. But, as it was with dreams, there was no true pain.

Ivy hummed, nuzzling into Vale's robes. She had never felt so held as she did in Vale's big arms. Why couldn't all her dreams be so sweet?

"You are awake," Vale said suddenly. "How do you feel?"

Ivy blinked, suddenly much more alert.

It wasn't a dream. She really was lying with Vale in his nest, plants swarming all around it. She sat up gingerly. As soon as she moved, the plants started to ripple. Petals fluttered, grass waved, vines bobbed and curled. For a moment, Ivy could feel their joy and relief and deep weariness. Then it faded, and Ivy was left reeling with her fuzzy memories.

Ivy looked up at Vale, stricken. "Did... did we go back to the mortal realm?"

Vale nodded. "Do you not remember?"

Ivy didn't answer. The memories were flooding back now, leaving her horrified: Vale carrying her forcefully back to the mortal realm; her uncle shooting her in the chest; her begging Vale not to kill her uncle, even after—oh *gods*.

Ivy covered her face with her hands. All those people, dead. She could remember their crumpled bodies now, lying where Vale had killed them.

Vale nosed at her hair. "What is it? You do not smell like pain."

"I got all those people killed," Ivy whispered.

Vale growled. "Your *uncle* got them killed. He almost killed *you*. You should have let me snap his neck."

"He's my *uncle*," said Ivy, appalled.

"He clearly does not value family as much as you," Vale replied. "Since he gave you to a Skullstalker, who he thought would eat you or ravish you against your will. And again, he *shot* you."

Ivy's chest throbbed. She looked down and saw a ragged hole in her dress. She had a small scar underneath it, pink and pitted. She touched it, thinking back to the blood that had stained her dress so badly. There was no blood now, although there was still the faint scent of it in the air. She wondered if Vale had washed her dress while she recovered, or if the void had magicked it away, like it had fixed her dress after Vale tore it in two.

"He didn't shoot me on purpose," Ivy muttered.

Vale huffed resentfully. Ivy almost wanted to join in. Her uncle might not have meant to shoot her, but he had thrown her away so easily! After all her work, all those years of trailing after him, talking people into their cause, washing pots and mending clothes and foraging for food... How could he give up on her like that? She never wanted to leave him. She just wanted him to not hurt Vale.

Cold dread washed over her as she remembered Vale's betrayed expression. He knew she had poisoned his void. That even if she was no longer helping her people to bind him, she was still the reason his void was dying.

But if he knew...

Ivy looked around the nest, all the plants watching her expectantly. Vale watched along with them, his gaze intense and, for some reason, caring.

"Why am I here?" Ivy asked.

Vale cocked his head. "You were injured."

"But..." Ivy's eyes itched. She forced the tears back, refusing to cry in front of him when she had ruined his life. "I poisoned your void. I was going to let him bind you to fight for us!"

"But you didn't," Vale said. "You tried to protect me. To talk your uncle out of his foolish plan. It was useless; he could not overpower me then, even with his malblossom. And you could not make him change his mind. He is blinded by his desires. I knew *that* when he gave you to me."

Ivy stared at him, stricken. Surely this couldn't be so easy. Whenever she ruined something in the Circle—burning a meal or botching a recruitment—she would, at the very least, get glared at.

But Vale wasn't glaring. He looked uncomfortable, those beautiful green eyes trained on his own claws, but there was no malice in his gaze.

Ivy watched the leaves twine around her shaking fingers. "How long will you let me stay here?"

Vale answered instantly. "You poisoned the pool."

Ivy winced. "Yes. I'm—"

"So, it is not your presence making it sick," Vale said, cutting her off.

Ivy waited. He couldn't be saying what she thought he was saying. Nobody had ever gotten pardoned from a crime so easily.

"So?" she said, finally.

"So, you do not need to leave," Vale said stiffly. "I told you. If it is not you, you can come back."

Ivy laughed wetly. He had said that when he was carrying her to the pool. It felt like a million years ago, though it had probably only been... hours? Days? Ivy had no idea how long she had been healing in this nest.

"You'd keep me here," Ivy said, stubborn tears spilling down her cheeks no matter how hard she tried to keep them back. "After what I did to you?"

"You are trying to fix it," Vale said, and paused. "If they came into my void right now—"

"I would die before letting them take you," Ivy said, shocking herself at the fierceness in her tone. She wiped her face, twisting in his arms to face him properly. "I will help you cure your void. I *will* fix my mistake. I *swear.*"

Vale made a rumbling noise deep in his throat and leaned down to kiss her.

Ivy gasped into his mouth. His lips were cool, but his mouth was blazing hot. He licked into her mouth, and Ivy groaned as her own tongue brushed against his razor-sharp fangs.

Vale grasped her face, tilting it sideways to kiss her deeper. His skull mask dug into her skin, his claws pressing hard against her soft cheeks. Ivy wondered if she would be covered in marks after. The idea filled her with a strange, fluttery zeal, much like when she touched the dents in her skin that he left behind from gripping her thighs while he sated her pollen-lust.

Suddenly, Vale pulled back, breathing hard. "You have no pollen in you. It would have bloomed in your blood again. It must have left you while you were healing."

"Oh," Ivy said, oddly disappointed. "I still want you. Is that... okay?"

Vale laughed and pressed a kiss to her forehead. "It will be good to mate you without the threat of your potential death. Will you still beg for me so sweetly?"

Ivy flushed. He licked her red cheek, then slipped his tongue into her mouth. Lightly at first, then deeper and deeper. Ivy opened obediently for him, heat pooling between her legs as he fucked his tongue further inside her mouth.

Finally, his tongue bumped the back of her throat. Ivy braced herself to gag. But her throat didn't reject him. If anything, it opened up—welcoming him in.

Ivy made a shocked noise, pushing at his chest.

Vale pulled his tongue out of her throat with a slick *pop*. He furled it back into his mouth, and Ivy shivered with want as she realized that it was slick with her own saliva.

"It must have worked," Vale said.

"What?" Ivy asked. Then another memory hit her, and she gasped. "The spell! You went to your brother?"

"I did."

"How does it work? Will I just...?" Ivy touched her throat. She had never managed to fit any man down her throat before, but her few attempts had left her drinking hot lemon water afterward. Her throat felt like it had nothing in it at all, let alone a Skullstalker's giant tongue less than a minute ago.

"I do not know," Vale admitted, his gaze trained hungrily on her. "Let us find out."

Thirteen

Ivy lay down in the nest, shivering with delight as Vale ran his hands over her dress.

It was actually very enjoyable to do this without the pollen. Before, she had been crazed with desire. Which was fun, but there was something wonderful about being able to luxuriate in his touch. His big, gentle hands stroking over her gauzy dress... His claws retracting as they slowly pushed the fabric up over her legs... His scarred fingers stroking her thighs...

Ivy frowned. Scarred fingers?

She sat up. Vale's hands were covered in healing burns.

"What happened to your hands?" Ivy asked, bewildered. Then she gasped, remembering the arrow he'd caught in midair. "The malblossom! Does the soothepine not work on burns?"

"It works on any wound," Vale said.

Ivy touched the back of his scarred palm. "Then why didn't you heal them?"

"I was busy," Vale said simply.

Ivy welled up again. She wiped her puffy cheeks, determined not to cry again. Then Vale ran his thumbs over her nipples, and Ivy let herself get lost in her growing arousal.

Vale nuzzled her thigh, where he'd pushed her dress up almost enough to expose her.

"Your scent drives me to distraction," he growled. "Every time the pollen began and your desire hung thick in the air, I was hardly able to keep working. But *you* kept working. You would squirm and pant and sweat. It would be all I could do not to pin you against the dirt and rut you until you screamed. You wanted to prove yourself to me. That you were worth keeping. Even when you thought I would be hauled out in a month."

Ivy averted her eyes. He grabbed her chin, forcing her to look down at him again.

"You did well," he said. "You are a good assistant."

Ivy smiled, stupidly proud. "You still want me as an assistant?"

Vale hesitated. His tail flicked behind him, then lowered to curl around her exposed ankle.

"You are more than that," he said. He didn't sound entirely happy about it.

Before Ivy could think why, Vale sat up, looming over her.

"You are connected to the void," he said. "It has *chosen* you.

It will not be content with you being a mere assistant. Neither would..."

He trailed off. His glowing eyes dropped to the plants crowding around the nest, flowers fluttering and vines writhing. Then he looked back at her, and his gaze went hungry.

"I can smell how wet you are," he said. He lifted his robes off, and Ivy's mouth dropped open as she saw his naked body outside of the river for the first time. Usually, he just took himself out of his robes. There was so much pale blue skin pulled strangely over his toned body. And, of course, his beautiful cock, hard and heavy, his shiny flat cockhead poking out from above the foreskin.

Ivy's mouth watered. She thought about pushing him back and taking him into her mouth, pushing that impossible length down her throat like he had done with his tongue. She had never sucked him before, always too desperate to get him inside her hole.

"Still so ready for me, even without the pollen," Vale continued, his voice dropping into a low, almost unintelligible rasp that made Ivy shiver. "Except if you still had the pollen, you would be begging by now."

"Please," Ivy said quietly.

Vale growled. "Beg better."

"*Please*," Ivy said, louder.

"You need better motivation," Vale told her.

Vines circled her wrists. Ivy twisted to look at them, smiling when they squeezed. Then the void's emotions leaked into her, and her smile faltered.

The void was tired. Scared. *Rotting*, slowly but surely. Then the vines squeezed again, and the fear and exhaustion were replaced by quiet excitement.

Ivy looked back at Vale. He stared down at her, his glowing eyes wide. He had felt the same thing, knotted into the same magic she was.

"Do we—" Ivy licked her lips. "Should we be doing something else? How are you feeling?"

"As good as I ever feel, these days," Vale said. He spared another glance at the plants wavering around them. "The void wants me to be with you. The void *always* wants me to be with you. And if what the mage said was true, and there is no antidote..."

His mouth hardened. He bent down, kissing her arrow scar and then moving up to her face, kissing her viciously.

Ivy kissed back, gasping as his fang tore into her lip. He lapped at the blood with a hungry noise and smeared his bloody lips down her neck.

"We can worry about our fate later," he said. "Open your legs."

Heart pounding, Ivy did. She had a vague wish that vines would grab her ankles, and just as the thought appeared, vines snaked around her ankles and pulled her legs wider apart.

Ivy grinned, biting her lip. She wasn't in *control* of the vines in the same way that Vale didn't control them. But they heard her. Even as tired as they were, they still wanted to please her. Or maybe it just wanted to touch her, Ivy considered as Vale pulled her dress up until she was exposed. Either idea made her tingle with desire.

Vale bunched her dress higher, nestling it over her breasts. He licked them, fangs grazing her nipples tantalizingly before pulling back to admire her.

"My strange little gift," he said. "All tied up for me."

"Come and have me," Ivy said, feeling very bold. Or maybe still full of adrenaline. She had been thrown out of the void and then shot by her uncle; she could be forgiven for feeling a little loopy.

Vale's cock throbbed, a bead of precum welling on his flat cockhead. He grabbed her waist and pulled her toward him, rubbing his cock against her hole.

Ivy moaned. For the first time since *the* first time, she wasn't sore. She almost missed it. But it was nice not to brace herself when he started pressing in.

For a moment, Ivy thought the spell hadn't worked. The stretch was still impossible, her entire body straining against it. But Vale's cock just kept going. In and in and *in*, not even needing to slowly work his way in with tiny thrusts like he'd been forced to do before. No tongue or fingers, or even a vine opening her up beforehand. Just a long, *long* slide, until he was pushing beyond where he usually stopped.

Ivy gasped, staring down at his cock as it slowly disappeared into her body.

Half his cock.

Two-thirds.

Then his balls were settling against her for the first time, both of them letting out wrecked noises as he bottomed out.

Ivy's stomach bulged. She gaped at it in disbelief. No wonder she couldn't fit all of him inside.

"You're so full of me," Vale groaned. "How does it feel? You do not smell like pain."

"It doesn't hurt," said Ivy faintly. She pulled at the vines around her wrists, suddenly wanting to touch the bulge of his cock inside her. She could feel every inch of him, her body barely stretching to fit. The spell must have... *rearranged* things. She should have been horrified. But she just wanted him to fuck her senseless.

Ivy stared up at him, her thighs shaking where they were being pulled apart by the vines. She felt wild with it, blood pumping, legs dripping with her own slick. She had no clue how she must smell to him right now, only that he would go feral over it.

"What else do I smell like?" she asked.

Vale growled. "*Mine.*"

He thrust again. Ivy watched as that gorgeous cock pushed in and out of her, filling her up in ways that were impossible this morning. Pleasure crackled through her core, and she squeezed her eyes shut against her will.

It felt so strange. It felt *incredible*. Like she'd been craving something her whole life and was only realizing now, while Vale fucked her faster and faster, his claws popping out as he lost himself in her.

"So soft," Vale panted, nuzzling her breasts. He fondled her stomach, running his claws over her folds. Ivy should have felt self-conscious, but it was difficult when his gaze was so reverent, his clawed hands coming up to stroke her cheeks and press into the softness like she was something worth keeping.

He had never touched her like this before. There were always moments, but he had never been so open about it. Never let her see how *hungry* he was for her.

The vines tightened around her wrists. The ones around her legs pulled her wider, spreading her open for him. Vale thrust harder, balls slapping loudly every time he pushed into the hilt.

Ivy heard herself whine. She had been concerned she wouldn't be able to let herself go without the pollen, but it turned out that she needn't have worried: Vale's inhuman cock could pull those noises out of her easily.

"I am close," Vale said raggedly.

Ivy's legs quivered in anticipation. She'd felt him come inside her before, but never *all* of him. What would it feel like, his whole length throbbing inside her as he came?

Vale opened his mouth, tongue lolling out. At first, Ivy thought he would circle her breasts again, or even shove down her throat. But Vale arched his head downward, his tongue slipping down over her stomach and the coarse hair covering her cunt, all the way down until it smeared over her clit.

Ivy arched up with a scream and came. She was dimly aware of his tongue still working at her, rubbing and even trying to fold around the tiny nub, his movements clumsy as his thrusts sped up.

She was riding out the last waves of her orgasm when he reared back and roared, spilling deep inside her.

Ivy felt all of it. Every lovely inch of him twitched with each spurt, filling her until his release gushed down her legs and puddled in the nest.

Vale collapsed on top of her, panting. The vines retreated from Ivy's limbs, and she ran a cautious hand over his antlers. His head twitched, and Ivy waited for him to pull away. But after a moment, he pressed his antlers harder into her grip.

"Well," Ivy said when she could breathe again. "The pollen is definitely gone."

Vale rumbled against her scalp.

"I kind of miss it," Ivy admitted. She thought about running her hands over all the places she had been too afraid to touch: his skull mask, the tips of his fangs, even his tail. But she didn't want to push her luck. He had let her touch his antlers; that had to be enough for now.

Vale rumbled louder, nuzzling her hair. "You could find another heatbloom."

Ivy laughed. It didn't last long.

"I don't know if we can afford to get distracted like that again," she said slowly.

Vale's face, lit up with amusement for once, dimmed instantly. He looked at the plants surrounding the nest, and Ivy wondered if he, too, felt the pulse of their exhaustion. Could he even untangle the void's tiredness from his own?

"What will we do?" Ivy asked him. "If there really isn't an antidote."

"We will make one," Vale said. But there was a hint of uncertainty in his tone. He had already asked all the Skullstalkers he knew. Skullstalkers were the oldest creatures Ivy knew of. If *they* didn't know, who else would?

"We could..." Ivy stopped, petting the vines that had been around her wrists. "We could find a way to sever you?"

Vale looked down at her gravely. He knew what she meant. But he was still going to make her say it.

"Sever me," Vale repeated.

The vine Ivy was petting nudged her hand. Like a dog asking for more affection, Ivy thought sadly. She didn't want to continue, but she couldn't live with herself if she didn't suggest it.

"So, you don't die with the void," Ivy whispered.

Vale answered just as she expected. "No. The void has been with me since the beginning. I will not—"

He went silent. His head snapped up, his glowing eyes darting around the trees.

Ivy sat up, alarmed. "What is it?"

Vale shook his head. He pulled his softening cock out of her, and Ivy gasped at the impossible slide. A flurry of emotions blurred through her until she couldn't tell which was hers and which was the void's: panic, pain, deep desire.

The forest shook.

Ivy braced herself against the nest, yanking her dress back into place over her sweaty skin. "What is it?"

"The pool," Vale growled.

He yanked on his robes. Then he grabbed her and slung her

onto his shoulder. Ivy grabbed his antlers, and Vale took off for the silver pool. Foliage shuddered and tried to bend out of the way, but always a moment too late. Ivy covered her face as sharp sticks caught her arms and tore her dress.

The ground went white under their feet. Vale stumbled, his claws sticking in the cracks. The poison had spread so much further than they thought.

Vale came to a stop, panting.

Ivy lowered her scratched arms and gasped.

The silver pool was empty.

Fourteen

Vale sat at the edge of the remnants of the silver pool, and his heart filled with dread.

Ivy sat beside him, gnawing her lip. "There's *some* water in it. Look there, down at the bottom."

She pointed. A thin layer of white sludge sat in the shallow depths of the hole. It stunk of poison and rot. If Vale stepped in it, the puddle would not even cover his toes, let alone transport him to another realm.

They were stuck in the wilderness void. Nobody could get in or out.

"Your Circle will be disappointed when they cannot get inside," Vale said.

"We were told the portal would *weaken*. Not... stop working," Ivy replied, peering into the useless hole miserably. Then she sat back, hugging her knees. "How do you feel?"

Vale resented the question. He was going to wither and die here, helpless. His lone companion would surely follow suit. Even without the bodily effects of the poison, how could he possibly feel anything but terrible?

"I am fine," he lied.

Ivy gave him a piteous look. She even reached out like she was going to touch his arm. Vale hoped she would. Vale hoped she would not. Before he could decide, her hand faltered and dropped back to her side.

"So, this is happening faster now," Ivy said, looking around them at the white, cracked ground that had spread so far around the pool. "We need to find some way out of this."

"Out of the void? There is none. Even if my brother tried to open a portal, he could not. The door is locked."

"No, I mean a way out of this situation." Ivy stood, curling her bare toes in the cracks the poison left behind. Her face twisted with regret, and Vale waited for her eyes to well. Then she took a deep breath, and her face smoothed out with determination.

"There is magic here," she started. "That even *you* don't understand. Right?"

She said it timidly, like he was worried he would be angry. But she still said it.

"I suppose," Vale said slowly. "But none that would allow us out of this void. Even if we found a way, where would we go? Our brothers do not know how to help. Your uncle insists there is no antidote."

"But we used a poison made in the mortal realm," Ivy said desperately. "Surely there's something here to counteract it!"

Vale stared glumly into the ruined pool, considering. It was harder to think with this exhaustion in his bones. "So, your solution is to pour every poison cure into the void until we fix it?"

"I don't know," Ivy sighed. "I just know we can't sit around here and let ourselves die! There's so much of this void I haven't seen. Maybe if we..."

She trailed off. She was silent for so long that Vale looked over at her, expectant.

She was not looking at him. She was staring at a flower on a nearby tree. It was white and wilting, succumbing to the poison. But it was still reaching for her.

Ivy walked over and touched its dying petal. It curled gingerly around her finger, then spasmed and went limp.

Ivy's breath hitched.

"What?" Vale demanded.

Ivy turned to him. Her eyes were glowing green. *His* green. The green of the wilderness void.

But only for a moment. Then the glow was gone, and her eyes were the beloved green that he had grown irritatingly attached to.

Ivy growled in frustration. "I lost it! It was trying to show me something, but it left before it could deliver the message. If I could find a way to connect with it, *really* connect with it, not just get thoughts and fleeting emotions, then maybe I could find a way to cure it."

"Maybe," Vale repeated, dubious. "What are you suggesting?"

Ivy tugged at her hair. It was up in a braid again—she had started braiding it out of stress as they sat by the useless pool.

"You know how you said I could spray myself with a heatbloom again?"

It took Vale a moment to remember. Their time in his nest felt like long ago, though it was possibly only minutes.

"You want to sicken yourself with pollen-lust," Vale said slowly. "*Now*?"

"Not for the lust! To talk to the void. The first time it sprayed me, that was when I heard it the loudest."

Vale was tired. Bone-deep, the kind of exhaustion that went beyond the physical. Part of him still felt betrayed that *he*, the one who had cared for the void all his long life, had not been communing with the void in place of this new mortal. But the anger was quieter now. It was harder to blame the void for reaching out to Ivy, who was filled with a passion he had been lacking for centuries.

"You think the pollen will let you connect with it more thoroughly," Vale finished.

Ivy smiled at him excitedly. "I think it can connect *us*."

"Us," Vale repeated. An idea formed in his head, golden and risky. "What do you mean?"

It did not take long to find a heatbloom. Just beyond the

rotting whiteness sat a strange plant that Vale had not seen in his void until Ivy appeared.

"You are sure about this?" Vale asked as he appraised the red flower the heatbloom had turned into upon Ivy's approach. "We will be insatiable."

"*I* will be insatiable," Ivy corrected. "For a while. You said the magic would be weaker with the poison. And you said it might not work on you."

"I have never caught it in its full force," Vale said warily. "I thought I felt *twinges* of its effects when I was wiping it off of you. But... that might have simply been from touching you."

He had not shared his emotions with any being for so long. It still felt wrong to do so. But less so with Ivy, who flushed with pleasure. The satisfaction it brought him to watch her smile was worth his reluctance to say it.

"Unless you have a better idea," Ivy said, toying with her braid. "I say we try it."

Vale inclined his head.

They stepped up together. Ivy reached out, and the plain red bloom twitched in response.

"The flower," Vale said. "What did you call it?"

Ivy's hand stopped. She looked up at him, surprised.

"A rose," she said. "They appear on the ivy here, sometimes. I don't know why. Back home, ivy doesn't have roses."

"It must be significant," Vale said. "The heatbloom only turns into something that lures you in."

Ivy said nothing. She looked oddly shy.

"I didn't know why at first," she admitted. "But now, I

think it's because of a storybook my mother read to me as a child."

"A storybook," Vale repeated. He had never heard of this.

"A book for children," she explained. "With pictures. It's about a gardener who falls for a princess. He sacrifices himself for her and dies. But she plucks the rose he grew for her and places it on his grave, and he comes back to life. That story was why I fell in love with plants in the first place. That illustration of a rose... It was so beautiful."

She grinned, her cheeks still red. Vale was, once again, struck by an annoying amount of want that he never had to bother with until she showed up. If this was what others had to contend with, he had no idea how they got any work done.

He wanted to tell her that she was gorgeous. But he had already complimented her a moment ago, and he was still not used to spilling his thoughts so often. So, he allowed her to step forward and touch the center of the rose.

It sprang open immediately. Vale was almost triumphant. His void might be sick, but it was not dead. And unlike him, it wanted loudly and unabashedly.

Pollen gushed out over them both. Vale closed his eyes, letting the warm fragrance wash over him. Golden motes stuck to his antlers and clung to his skull mask, showering over his robes and the exposed part of his chest.

Finally, the torrent ended. Before Vale even had time to open his eyes, he heard a gasp beside him.

He blinked pollen out of his eyes and looked over.

Ivy was radiant. The pollen did not just cover her—it

adorned her. Tangling in her braid-crown and dusting her fair skin, making her body shine. She looked like a creature from a myth.

"Do you feel it?" she asked breathily.

Vale concentrated. He could not feel the pollen's influence. He *could* feel the void, but only faintly. He could only catch glimpses of its exhaustion, nothing of the words it had been sending him sporadically since Ivy showed up.

"No," he replied. "Can you?"

She nodded, her smile trembling. "It's... *wonderful*. I can... I can almost..."

She stumbled into his arms. Her hands caught on his chest, smearing pollen. And suddenly, he was seized by a wild desire unlike anything he had felt before. It made his entire body clench, a growl tearing out of his throat.

His exhaustion vanished as the world narrowed down to Ivy. Her slick skin and her even slicker thighs, still dripping with him from their last coupling. Her hot breath against his chest, her skin heavy with pollen. She was moaning, grinding against his leg like an animal in heat.

"Have me again," she gasped, eyes still glowing green. "I'm close."

Vale did not know if she meant she was close to her peak or to finding answers to the void. But he did not care. He cared for nothing but Ivy, the only thing he had truly wanted in centuries.

He pushed her to her knees and yanked their clothes out of the way, then shoved unceremoniously inside her. He had mated her less than an hour ago, but they both groaned like it had been an eternity. His spend slicked the way, but even without it, the slide was easy. Her inner walls strained and squeezed but never protested—even when he pushed all the way to the hilt.

Ivy went lax, moaning into the dirt. There were no vines to hold her down, but Vale made do. He grabbed her hands, listening to her breathing hitch in excitement as he pinned them behind her back.

He could not get close enough. He licked salt from her neck and golden pollen from her cheek, his tongue curling around her throat. If he were not so pollen-crazed, he would have worried he was taking her too roughly—even more roughly than he allowed himself before. But there was no pain in her scent, only desire so wet it squelched each time he drove back in.

"Yes," Ivy slurred into the dirt. "Yes, I'm—I'm so *close*—"

She cut off with a cry. It turned strange and otherworldly, almost a howl as green light radiated out of her, overshadowing the golden pollen coating her skin.

Vale thrust one last time and came, pumping deep inside. He slumped over her, his hands trembling around her wrists as the pollen-lust faded from his blood.

Ivy hummed tiredly. Vale circled an arm around her waist and dragged her up, dusting the dirt from her cheek where it had been pressed into the ground.

"What did you see?"

Ivy looked up at him, almost bending backwards to do so.

Her eyes were bright from the green void-glow. But it faded fast, leaving only her natural green behind.

"The vial that hangs from my uncle's staff," she declared. "That's the antidote! *Hells*! We could have grabbed it off of him!"

Vale was suddenly glad that he hadn't crushed that irritating vial when he had the chance. There had been several times where he had considered it, watching it swing infuriatingly with each movement of the staff.

"We will," Vale said, stroking a claw down her pollen-heavy neck. "If we manage to find our way into the mortal realm."

Ivy's grin grew. She sat up, gasping as he slid out of her. Then she turned to him, so full of giddy confidence that Vale had to stop himself from kissing her.

"The void isn't just dying," she said delightedly. "It's *breaking*."

"I take it there is a reason you are happy about that."

Ivy nodded, her disheveled braid falling out of place from its circle atop her head. "It's *breaking*! That means there are *cracks*."

"Into other realms," Vale realized. "And if we find a crack to the mortal realm—"

"We can get through and find the cure!" Ivy yelled. She stood, her pollen-stained dress falling back down her legs as she whooped and jumped. She whirled in a circle, arms outstretched. Trees bent weakly to touch her, leaves leaping from their branches to touch her skin on the way to the ground.

Vale watched her, spellbound. He had never seen anything

so beautiful. If only he had the time to appreciate it. Then again, if her plan worked, they could have more time than he dreamed. If he fixed the silver pool, one of their first stops after hunting down that vial would be to his Anderfel brother to extend Ivy's lifespan to match his own.

Vale climbed to his feet. At first, all was well, still feeling the rush of the pollen. Then his head swam, and he hit the ground once more.

Ivy stopped spinning and knelt in front of him, concerned. "Vale?"

She grabbed his arm. She could not pull him up. She could not even steady him. But Vale appreciated the effort.

Vale pushed himself to his feet again. His vision swam, and his legs threatened to give out again, but he held firm until the dizziness passed.

"The crack to the mortal realm," he said. "Do you know where it is?"

Ivy nodded wildly.

"Good," Vale said. "Lead the way."

Fifteen

It had been three days of walking, and Ivy's feet still weren't sore.

Ivy ran her hand over her heel as she sat on a bony tree trunk. The skin was soft and pink, nothing like what she would have expected. She had been a nomad for most of her life. Trekking through forests, mountains, and the like. The only reason her feet were so soft when she entered the wilderness void was because her uncle insisted on it.

You must be a good offering, he had said as he handed her a rough stone to sand down her tough feet during her last bath. *Something worth taking.*

Ivy's lip curled. She forced the memory away and stood, flexing her toes in the dark dirt.

"Vale," she called. "Are you ready? We should keep going."

No reply. Ivy craned her head, trying to spot him through

the dense trees. The white rot had not reached this far into the void, and everything was still dark and lush.

"Vale?"

Still no response. Ivy chewed her lip and reached inside her head for the void. However, before she could sense anything but its ever-present exhaustion, she heard heavy footsteps through the trees.

Vale stepped through the bushes carrying a handful of frostberries.

"For you," he said.

Ivy beamed, ridiculously pleased. Frostberries didn't grow in the small area where she had been working those first few weeks. They had only stumbled on them on their last day of walking. Even though Ivy was connected to the void, she had explored so little of it.

"Thank you," Ivy said. She took a frostberry and popped it into her mouth, enjoying the firm, icy texture. It reminded her of the ice cream they ate sometimes back at the castle, the childhood memory so hazy she sometimes thought she dreamed it.

Vale kept walking. Ivy walked beside him, eating out of his hand. The void pulsed in her head, alerting her that they were almost at their destination. But before she could say it, Vale spoke up.

"We are almost there," Vale announced.

Ivy paused, covering her mouth to hide the frostberry she was chewing. "How do you know?"

"I may not have the void talking in my ear anymore," Vale said. "But I remember where the castle is."

Ivy nodded, feeling silly. Vale had been here for millennia; of course, he knew where everything was.

"It was on your list of things to fix," Ivy said, taking another frostberry from his cupped palms. "Right? Clearing up the castle?"

Vale grunted. "I do not think we will have time to clean."

Ivy laughed. It was shorter than usual. She was distracted by his gait, which was slumped and slow. His eyes were a dull glow. And were his claws more brittle than yesterday? She would try to check when the pollen took over later. He enjoyed digging his claws into her hips.

They were down to the last few frostberries when Vale growled out of nowhere.

"Stop looking at me like that."

Ivy startled, tearing her probing gaze away. "Like what?"

"With pity in your eyes," Vale said.

"There's no pity," Ivy tried. "I'm just worried."

"Do not worry. There is no sense in it."

Ivy stared up at the trees. Even though the rot had not reached them yet, the leaves were fading. The bony tree trunks chipped at the slightest touch. The entire void was weakening, and Vale weakened with it.

"We can walk slower," Ivy offered.

"We cannot," Vale replied. "We must cure the void."

Ivy plucked the last frostberry from Vale's hands, irritated as she chewed. She couldn't argue with that logic. But she hated forcing him onward when he was feeling like this.

"Do not frown," Vale said, dropping his berry-stained

hands. "I have been working tirelessly for generations before you were born."

"Yes," Ivy said hesitantly. "And you shouldn't have. I can't believe the void didn't make you more light-motes!"

The void stirred in her head. It did not feel offended, like Ivy had been worrying about. She wondered if she could offend the void at all. If poisoning the void didn't upset it, then this certainly wouldn't.

"It cannot," Vale said. "That is surely the only reason it would not give me more."

Ivy nodded thoughtfully. It made sense. But it also filled her mind with questions.

"Where did they come from in the first place?" she asked. "The light-motes?"

"I do not know. They simply appeared." Vale came to a stop, his face creasing in pain. It was the most she had seen him react beyond falling down, and Ivy touched his elbow in alarm.

"What's wrong?"

"Nothing new." Vale dropped his head, his glowing eyes squeezing shut as he braced himself through whatever was roiling through him. Then he opened his eyes and started walking again, his shoulders slumped and his tail dragging on the ground.

"Speak to me," he said as Ivy dropped into step beside him. "Distract me from these annoyances."

Ivy couldn't help but smile. Mere weeks ago, *she* had been the annoyance. He'd told her to stop talking many times. Now he was asking for it.

"Of course," Ivy said. Then she paused. "I can't think of anything. What do you want me to say?"

"Tell me of your Circle."

Ivy stumbled over a rock. She righted herself quickly, matching her stride to Vale. She didn't want to think about the Circle. When she did, her thoughts went back to those whom Vale had killed the last time they were in the mortal realm.

"Well," she said hesitantly. "The ones you killed weren't very nice. So that's... good?"

Vale rumbled threateningly. "You should have told me. I would have spent longer killing them."

"They weren't awful," Ivy said. "They just weren't *nice*. None of them were, really. At least, not to me. It was... strange, actually. Someone at one of the last towns we passed through said they made me a scapegoat for all that went wrong. I did make a lot of mistakes, but not enough to deserve my treatment. Or so they said. Now that I think back on it..."

Ivy bit her lip. "My uncle might have been behind it? I felt so silly for even suspecting it back then. But I kept hearing him say bad things about me behind my back, like he wanted the others to think less of me. Maybe he wanted me to rely on him. He was the only one who was nice to me, even if he did treat me like a servant. I thought I just needed to work harder, you know? Prove myself. Be *useful*."

She fell silent, embarrassed. She had never said it aloud before. She'd never had anyone to say those words to.

Vale did not speak for several steps. At first, Ivy thought he was too lost in his pain or that he had nothing to say.

"You need not do that for me," he said finally.

Ivy couldn't help it: she laughed. She had spent these past few weeks working every moment of the day, save for sleep and slaking her pollen-lust. If anything, Vale had told her to work harder. She couldn't even blame him. Everywhere they went was full of work to be done.

"You do *not*," Vale insisted. "It is necessary now, with all the work that is to be done. But if you stay here, in my void... I can find other assistants. I *will* find others."

Ivy stared up at him in shock. "Really? Even... even after how finding your first assistant went?"

"I did not find you. You were given to me." Vale walked several more paces, his tail swishing. Then he stopped and turned to her, taking her chin in his berry-stained claws.

"You deserve a life," he said. "Not just work."

The words were for her. But there was confusion in his voice, as if he was only just realizing that the same might even apply to him.

Ivy's heart fluttered. She was so distracted by Vale's intense gaze that she barely noticed that, yes, his claws were more brittle than the day before.

He tilted her chin up and kissed her. It was cool and soft and sweet, despite his fangs grazing her lip.

The pollen stirred inside Ivy's blood. But before it could properly bloom, Vale grunted and pulled back.

Ivy stroked his mossy cheekbone. "How badly does it hurt?"

Vale didn't answer. He twisted away from her, craning his head to peer through the trees.

"We are here," he announced, and stalked forward.

Ivy followed. The trees came to an abrupt stop, and Ivy gasped as she saw the view waiting beyond them.

The castle had been rotting for a long time, aged bone crumbling into what was once a moat. It was even bigger than it had looked when the void pushed images into her head. Even bigger than the castle she had lived in as a child, bigger than any castle mortals could create. The ruined spires looked like they could scrape the sky. The doors were crafted from bone, so big and heavy, she doubted even Vale could heave them open. Luckily, there was a chunk missing in the bone big enough for both of them to walk through.

The void pushed another weak image onto her: giant beings fighting in the courtyard. *Titans*. A war before the Skullstalkers even existed, let alone mortals. An ancient siege machine, taking a chunk of the door. Then the image was gone, and she was alone in her head again.

Ivy reeled, holding her pounding head.

Vale stepped back toward her. "Ivy?"

"I'm fine," she gasped. She shook her head, the void's memories already fading.

Vale held out his hand.

Ivy took it, and the two of them set off toward the hole punched in those impossibly huge doors.

Sixteen

Vale watched Ivy stare around the wide, bony walls. He should have urged her to walk faster. To follow where the void was directing her. But he was so tired, and Ivy looked so lovely as she gazed wondrously around the crumbling castle.

"Is it very different?" Vale asked.

Ivy laughed, running her hand over a chipped wall. "For one, mortal castles are made of *stone*, not bone. And they're not as big. Or abandoned. Or..."

She trailed off, her eyes flashing green as they came to a stop in front of a towering doorway.

Vale peered inside, ignoring the exhaustion pounding through his marrow.

The throne room had decayed since he last saw it several decades ago. A new hole had opened in the ceiling, allowing vines to creep through and twine down the painted wall and over the twin thrones sitting side by side against the rear wall. Once, there had been a giant skeleton sitting slumped on one of those thrones. It had been the first thing Vale cleared.

Vale turned to Ivy. "Is it here?"

"I…" Ivy cleared her throat, the green glow draining from her eyes. "I think so." She pointed at the painted wall behind the thrones. "What is that?"

Vale looked up at the faded painting. It was partially obscured by vines, but there was enough showing through to make it clear: a rich, lush, bony wonderland.

"That is the void when it is healthy and taken care of," Vale said. "It looked like this when I still had the light-motes to assist me."

Ivy pointed higher up the wall. "And those?"

Vale lifted his gaze. This was why he had stayed away from the castle these past few centuries. He did not want to look at the hazy, gleaming lights floating above the content void, even in a painting—dozens of them dancing in the dark sky, beautiful and joyous.

"Those are the light-motes," he said quietly.

Ivy tilted her head, her braid falling down her cheek. "Did they have names?"

She said it dreamily, like she already knew the answer. He said it anyhow.

"Yes," he admitted.

She did not ask. He was glad for it.

"You lost your joy," she murmured, her eyes huge and green

once more. Her voice became strange and deep. "*The caretaker must be fulfilled. Or they wither.*"

Vale startled. "What?"

Ivy shook her head. The glow faded from her eyes.

"Huh? I don't—" Ivy rubbed her forehead. "I'm sorry. I don't know what that was."

Vale reeled at the implications. He *had* been happy before the light-motes died. Had he not? He always thought that his joy vanished with the light-motes. But was it the other way around? Did they vanish because he was dissatisfied?

"It *is* in here," Ivy said. "At least, that's what the void says."

Vale pushed his thoughts of ancient history aside and stepped inside the throne room, looking around for a crack in the void that would allow them into the mortal realm. The thrones were decaying, as were the walls. The paint was so faded that it was difficult to make out under the vines crawling over it. But there was nothing that looked like a gap in the void.

"I do not see anything," Vale said.

"I don't *feel* anything," Ivy agreed, her voice faint. She cleared her throat again, and Vale noticed how red her cheeks were. He thought it was because of the walking. But this was different from the flush that cropped up when they had been walking for several hours. This flush traveled into her dress, making her hot under the flimsy fabric. Making her *wet*.

Vale inhaled deeply. The sweet scent of her slick made him feel as if the pollen was rising inside him again, even though his pollen had left his blood on the first day.

"You feel *something*," he corrected, stepping closer. He wound his tail around her leg, and Ivy stuttered a laugh.

"Can't go into pollen-heat when we rush the mortal realm," she said. She turned to him, warm and rosy with her lust. "We have to be fast."

"That is never a problem with you," Vale assured her.

Ivy laughed again. There was something desperate underneath it, as there always was when the pollen set in.

She reached for him. Vale bent obligingly, capturing her in a kiss. He had never kissed so much until she came along. He assumed it was a mortal preference. But now he could not get enough of it: her tender mouth, her hungry tongue. The way she panted against him, never shying away from his fangs as he expected her to. Even when she had not been under the influence of the pollen, she had not shied away from them.

Something began to glow. Vale opened his eyes to see her eyes glowing behind their lids, even as she continued to kiss him.

Ivy broke away, chest heaving.

"*The throne*," she said, her eyes glowing, her voice strange and deep once more.

Vale frowned. Was the void... *speaking* through her? It never sounded like that in his head, but he could come up with no other explanation.

Ivy shuddered, her eyes going back to normal. "Sorry! The throne... We need to be on the throne."

She pushed at him. Vale walked back, settling on the smaller throne. It was covered in uncomfortable vines, but he did not care. Not when Ivy was sitting on his lap, grinding against him like she was already close.

"Please," she said, pulling her dress up. "Vale, I *need* it."

Vale reached for his robes, pulling his cock free through the fabric. A not-insignificant part of him wanted to push her over the arm of the throne and mate her like that. But he *was* exhausted, and Ivy seemed just as happy to stand up on his lap and sink down on his cock.

They groaned in unison as he filled her. Ivy was so short she had to squat, taking a mere half of him before she stood back up, legs trembling.

Then she sat down. His cock filled her so thoroughly that it bulged in her stomach every time she lowered herself.

Vale gripped her hips, taking care not to dig his claws through her dress.

Ivy stared up at him, her face slack. "H-harder."

Vale snapped his hips up. Ivy groaned, her head falling into his chest. For a moment, all she could utter were choked-off moans. Then she lifted her head, her cheeks so pretty and pink, Vale had to kiss her.

Ivy moaned against his lips, then pulled away. "Your claws. Do it harder."

At first, Vale did not understand. But he tightened his claws experimentally, checking her reaction.

Ivy's eyelids fluttered. She let out a cry, riding him faster.

Vale pressed his face to her hair, inhaling deeply. There was a hint of bitter pain underneath her sweet pleasure. But if anything, it only made the desire smell more enticing. Ivy certainly seemed to think so, her moans reaching a fever-pitch as she rode him.

Vale thought that she had been suffering through the pain for the sake of her pleasure. Now he understood what had been missing since he cast the spell that allowed her to take all of him, no pain required. The pain was part of her enjoyment.

Vale dug his claws in deeper. Blood trickled into her dress, and Ivy giggled. It was such an unexpected response to bloodshed that Vale could not help but marvel at her. His strange little offering, who wormed her way into his life with the intent to destroy it, only to go against her people to help him save everything he held dear.

It made him want to slow down. To quieten the eager rocking of her hips, to bask in her closeness. But the pollen was working its magic inside her, filling her with desperation to climax as fast as possible. So Vale reached down and rubbed at her instead, urging the process along.

Ivy yelled and stilled, trembling in his arms. Then she sagged, and the scent of pollen faded into her usual sweetness.

Vale took his claw tips out of her hips, ignoring the hunter-brain that awakened within him at the scent of blood. He lifted her up and down on his still-hard cock.

Ivy moaned weakly. She squeezed around him, always so eager to please.

"You will stay here," Vale said into her hair. "Be my queen. That is partly why your uncle sent you, yes? In the hopes I would lift you to godhood."

"I wouldn't call having a—*ohhh*—a void in my head *godhood*," Ivy panted, grinning.

Vale nuzzled her sweaty skin. Then he took her chin, tilting it back until she was staring at him while he lifted her easily up and down.

"I never wanted power," Ivy said. "That was my uncle. I just wanted—*oh*!"

She cut off with a cry, her eyes slamming shut. Pleasure, of course. But also magic. The void's green glow leaked out from her eyelids, seeping through her face and shining from her chest.

"You wanted?" Vale prompted, thrusting faster. His completion was rushing toward him, undeniable now.

Ivy let out another shaky laugh. The green light was brighter now, but it did not matter. Vale saw her perfectly: her wonky braid and her flushed cheeks and her beautiful face naked with desire.

"I just wanted to find a place that wanted me," she admitted.

Vale pushed as deep as he could and came with a weak growl. It was not a powerful orgasm, but still enough to make his legs shake. Although apparently even walking could do that these days.

Ivy's green glow dimmed. Vale pulled back to ask if she had seen something, only to pause as he noticed her hips.

Her dress had fallen over them again. The gauzy material was stained red with tiny dots where he'd sunk his claws in.

Vale brushed them gently. "I can find some soothepine."

"Don't bother." Ivy touched the small wounds, her fingers fitting between his claws. "I quite like them. The sensation is exciting. And, well… if they scar, then it's like I'm yours."

"You do not need a scar to remind you of that," Vale assured her. "You were given to me, and I am keeping you."

Ivy beamed, her eyes filling. She opened her mouth, then stopped, her gaze fixing on something behind his head.

Vale turned to see the wall behind them flickering.

Ivy gasped. "The painting!"

She climbed off his softening cock and stumbled onto the bone floor, walking around the thrones to reach the glowing circle that had appeared across the wall.

"It's in the middle of the light motes," Ivy said. She reached up, ghosting her hand over the glow that would have matched the painted creatures if the paint was not so faded. Then she turned to grin at Vale, who was still sitting on the throne.

"This has to be it! Come on, let's go find the antidote!"

Vale heaved himself off the throne and went to her side. He attempted to walk as he always did, but Ivy's sagging smile proved otherwise.

"How are you feeling?" she asked.

His least favorite question. Vale sighed, his tail lifting grudgingly. The temporary energy from having Ivy on top of him was gone, leaving only the void's exhaustion behind. If the mortals wanted to make him easier to bind, they had their wish.

"I can still fight," he said.

Ivy did not look comforted by his words. Vale scooped her up, settling her in his arms. He took one last look at the faded painting he was about to step into, his long-gone light-motes forming a circle of light for them. Almost as if they had been waiting.

"We will find your uncle," Vale announced. "We will retrieve the antidote. We will kill anyone who gets in our way."

Ivy squirmed uncomfortably in his grip.

Vale's eyes narrowed. "If you did not want me to kill your Circle, you should not have told me they were cruel to you."

"They weren't *that* bad," Ivy protested.

Vale sighed. "We will only kill people who try to kill us first."

Ivy kissed his chin. "Good. Now let's go save our void."

The words sent a fissure of rightness through Vale's heart.

He tightened his grip on Ivy, then he stepped out of the wilderness void.

Seventeen

Ivy clung to Vale's neck as they stepped out into a dark forest.

She barely held herself back from whooping as she recognized the pine trees. They were in the mortal realm! And from the look of the markings carved in the trees that were only used by the Circle to keep track of where they had been, they were on the Circle's trail.

Ivy looked up at Vale and whispered, "Can you hear anything?"

Vale shushed her. His head was cocked, his tail swishing.

The green portal glowed behind him. Ivy craned her head and saw that they had emerged through a gnarled tree. The tree looked familiar, and Ivy blinked in shock as she spotted a stone slab in the distance.

They weren't just close to the Circle. They were close to the place she had been offered to Vale. To the place Vale had been summoned.

"They're here," Ivy whispered. "Right? What are they trying to do?"

Vale shook his head and started to creep forward. For such a large creature, he was shockingly light on his feet.

The green portal sealed shut behind them. Ivy bit her cheek to stop herself from swearing. How would they get back?

Ivy's uncle's voice drifted through the trees. Light followed it, and Ivy squinted until she could make out a large campfire burning in the middle of a clearing. The Circle was gathered around it, Christopher in the center with his robed arms raised.

Ivy strained to look. He wasn't holding his staff, and the vial that was usually tied to it was nowhere to be seen.

"He doesn't have the vial," Ivy whispered. "Do you think he's hiding it?"

Vale shushed her.

"We gather here tonight to mourn our brothers and sisters," Christopher yelled to the Circle. "And to avenge them! Together, we will bind the monster that took them from us and bend him to our will. By now, our poison will have weakened him so much we might as well carry him out with our bare hands!"

A cheer went up. Christopher raised his robed arms higher, and Ivy frowned. He was wearing a strange headdress, one he only brought out for powerful spells. They were clearly planning something big.

"They mean to break into the void by force," Ivy whispered. "Can they do that?"

"Not without an immense amount of power," Vale replied. "More than any lone mortal has."

"What's our plan?"

Vale said nothing. He crept around the tree line, making sure to stay far away from the distant campfire light.

Ivy stayed quiet, calculating their next moves. She couldn't fight, let alone do magic. Vale was weakened. Could they lure her uncle away and ambush him? All they needed was the vial. Surely, it was on his person. He wouldn't let something that important out of his sight.

Vale continued to creep through the trees. Not toward the Circle, but around them. Was he flanking them?

"Where are we going?" Ivy whispered.

After a moment, Vale stopped. "Here."

Ivy looked up.

There was a cage waiting in the dark. Hastily constructed, with fire spells melting the metal together. The bars of the cage were lodged deep in the ground and were covered in thin, flowery vines.

Ivy peered closer. Those weren't just any flowery vines; they were the distinctive white petals of malblossom.

A cage for Vale, Ivy thought, her heart sinking. Then Vale carried her closer, and the moonlight revealed what the cage was truly for.

The Skullstalker, who was currently inside.

At first, Ivy thought it was just a man. A large man, but still just a man restrained with malblossom-infused rope. He was so much smaller than Vale that she didn't realize it was a Skullstalker until she saw the blue tinge of his skin and the skull mask attached to his face. He was struggling, grunting in pain as his flowery bindings scored his skin.

"Brother," Vale hissed.

The Skullstalker froze. Then he twisted, and Ivy gasped in sympathy as she saw his glowing purple eyes. One of them was swollen shut, a malblossom still burning his eyelid where it hung over his face. He also had one horn broken off.

"Brother," said the small Skullstalker, so loud and joyous they both shushed him.

Ivy whispered, "You know him?"

"I have never spoken to him," Vale said. "But he has spoken to Slate and our Anderfel brother. He was asking them for a wife."

"Or a husband," said the small Skullstalker eagerly. "I am not picky."

Something shifted behind his back. Ivy was shocked to see a big fuzzy tail attempting to wiggle where it was bound to his back.

"I am Zax," the small Skullstalker announced. "What are your names?"

"I am Vale," Vale said quietly.

"Vale!" Zax repeated, seemingly more bothered with introductions than getting his burning restraints off him. "And who is this? Is this your wife? What is your wife's name?"

"Her name is Ivy," Vale said.

Ivy's heart skipped a beat. Vale had offered to make her his queen; maybe she shouldn't be so enthralled at the idea of him calling her his wife. Wait, *was* she his wife now? She was part of the void, but he would tell her if they were Skullstalker-married. Right?

"Ivy!" Zax whispered, his tail still attempting to wag despite the ropes. "Hello!"

"Hello," said Ivy, reluctantly charmed.

Vale stepped closer to the cage, placing Ivy down on the ground. Ivy glanced over at the campfire, where her uncle was still riling up the Circle and paying no attention to the Skullstalker they had caught.

"If they've already caught a Skullstalker, why do they need to break into your void for you?" Ivy asked.

"For a bigger army," Vale replied.

Ivy got down on her knees and crawled forward until she could touch the bars on the Skullstaker's cage. "How did they capture you?"

"Nets," Zax said. "Lots of them. It *really* hurts."

"I know, we'll get you out of that soon." Ivy winced at the smoke rising off Zax's blue skin. "But what magic did they use to capture you?"

Vale bent down low behind her. "None. He is young. Small. They are easier to take down than older Skullstalkers. They will only need to prepare a spell to bind him to their commands when they send him to fight their battles."

Ivy nodded. She pulled thoughtfully at the malblossom around the cage, then looked beseechingly up at Vale.

"I can get rid of the malblossom," she whispered as her uncle droned on in the background about rights and destiny. "Can you lift the cage out of the ground?"

Vale flexed, his arm muscles straining his robes. "I can try."

He looked dubious. Ivy wondered just how weak he felt right now. How the void fared without them around to care for it.

She turned back to the cage and started pulling malblossom away from the cage, making sure to be quiet every time she snapped a vine.

"They said they are going to use me in their battles," Zax told them. "I like to hunt. When something runs from me, I chase it down and kill it. I might have joined their battle for fun. But not after they have done this. Now I will kill them all!"

"We will help," Vale assured him.

Ivy kept plucking the malblossom off the cage bars. She wanted to protest, but she would save that for later. Right now, she had to focus on finding the antidote and getting it to the void.

Finally, she stripped enough malblossom for Vale to grip the cage bars. She stood back, tensing as Vale slowly started to pull.

One inch of the cage slid out of the ground. Then another. Vale's face creased, growling quietly as he strained. Ivy waited for the group to turn around and notice, but they were too busy staring at her uncle, enraptured. Waiting.

Several bars of the cage came free. Vale lifted it, and Ivy crawled underneath them and started yanking at the malblossom ropes.

"I need something sharp," she told Vale.

He grunted with the effort of holding the cage up. Then he lifted one hand off and snapped a claw from his thumb.

"Thanks," Ivy whispered, and went back to work.

It did not take much sawing for Zax to snap the rest of the ropes and stumble up.

"Thank *you*," he told Ivy, still sounding much too delighted for a creature with his eye swollen shut and burns over most of his body.

They crawled out from under the cage. Vale let the bars drop back into the ground. His knees wobbled, and Ivy touched his shoulder worriedly.

"I am fine," he assured her. But he was breathing hard, sweat pricking his pale skin as he stared over Ivy's shoulder and pointed.

Ivy turned. Her uncle had produced the top half of his staff, broken from his last encounter with Vale, and he was thrusting it in the air. Tied to the top of the broken staff, dangling and gleaming in the firelight, was—

"The antidote," Ivy hissed. "We need to find some way to get it off of him without alerting the others! We could... We could make a noise to lead him away?"

"He would send his followers," Vale argued.

Ivy sighed, crouching behind the cage, her mind churning. The vial was right *there*. If they could only...

Something curled over her bare foot.

Ivy barely held back a yelp. She looked down and was shocked to spot a line of ivy working over her toes.

Zax made a strange chirping noise. "Are *you* doing that?"

Ivy looked up at Vale. He inclined his head as if to say, *Well, I'M not doing it.*

"I guess so," Ivy whispered.

Zax cocked his head, his remaining eye squinting down at the ivy as it slid over Ivy's foot. "We could tie *him* up. How much ivy do you have? How fast can you—oh! *Ivy*! It has your name! Is that why you command it?"

"Um, sort of," Ivy whispered, and turned back to the group crowded around the fire. Her uncle dropped his staff to his side, the antidote hanging perilously close to the ground.

Ivy took a deep breath. Then she extended a hand out to the ivy and willed it forward.

The ivy climbed over the forest floor, growing at a rate Ivy gaped at. Every moment brought a new stretch of vine, more leaves sprouting as it neared the Circle.

"Do not go straight through," Vale said.

"I have it," Ivy replied. The ivy was already curving around the group, edging around the campfire light before approaching Christopher from the side.

"Slowly," Vale said.

"I *have* it," Ivy repeated.

She flexed her fingers. The ivy crept up toward her uncle, his staff still dangling at his side as he yelled.

"Everyone," he called. "It's time to cast the evocation! Prepare yourselves to receive my magic."

"What is it?" Zax asked.

"He's—" Ivy frowned. "He's casting a spell on *them*? Why would he do that?"

"Ivy," Vale said.

She shushed him, peering closer. But before she could make out the symbol, Vale's knee gave out. He crumbled to the forest floor, breathing hard.

"Vale!" Ivy abandoned her creeping plant and touched his face, wiping away the sweat. "Oh, gods. How bad is it?"

"The... void..." Vale coughed, his lip curling in annoyance as his body failed him. "It is dying."

"What?" Ivy thought back to the white rot spreading from the silver pool. "But... but it hasn't spread that far! We have time!"

"We do not," Vale said, every breath an effort. He forced himself up, bracing his elbows in the dirt. "Do not worry about me. Focus on the antidote."

Eyes burning, Ivy turned back to the Circle. She stretched out her hand, and the ivy that had stopped just before her uncle's boot began to climb his robes.

"Remember," Christopher yelled over the crowd, oblivious to the ivy stretching up the back of his robes. "This spell might make you feel weak! But never fear, your energy will return to you."

"Ivy," Vale gritted.

"I know!" Ivy focused back on the plant creeping up her uncle's robes, her hands shaking with effort. Her uncle always said using magic was exhausting, but she had never felt it before.

Even in so much danger, it filled Ivy with a thrill. The void had changed her to her marrow.

"When I cast this spell," Christopher continued as Ivy watched the vines creep up his arm, "You will be able to move through the door I once summoned the Skullstalker through! Do not be alarmed by whatever horrors you encounter. Focus on restraining the monster—another weapon for our army to take back our rightful place!"

A cheer rippled through the crowd. Ivy frowned. They needed a spell to move through the door? What was he talking about? That didn't sound like any spell Ivy knew. Why focus on the people and not the barrier itself?

"And revenge," Christopher bellowed, his eyes bright with firelight as the ivy climbed his arm. "On the beast who took our people from us!"

The cheer grew louder. Christopher thrust his broken staff into the air, and Ivy grimaced. She was *almost* there. She directed it further up Christopher's arm, sweat beading on her scalp. The vine was climbing the staff now. Just a few more inches until she reached the vial...

Christopher shook the staff, making the ivy shake with it. "Expose your symbols!"

The Circle yanked down their shirts. A strange circular symbol had been drawn over their hearts with clay. It looked so strange that Ivy frowned, almost forgetting to concentrate on the ivy creeping toward the staff.

She might not be a mage like her uncle, but those symbols on everyone's chests did not look like they were going to do anything *to* them. It looked like it was going to do something *with* them.

"He's lying," Ivy realized. "He's not casting a spell *on* them. He's using them *in* a spell."

"To do what?" Zax demanded.

Ivy didn't answer. She had a horrible suspicion, but her uncle couldn't be capable of *that*. Right?

"Ivy," Vale panted.

"I'm almost there," Ivy replied. But she reached down with her spare hand to squeeze his claws.

He batted her hand away and touched her collarbone. At first, Ivy was confused, thinking he was tracing a symbol into her chest like her uncle had gotten his followers to do. Then it struck her. He wasn't tracing a symbol; he was tracing her *scar*. The one her uncle had caused when he shot a bolt into her chest.

"Glory is coming," Christopher bellowed, the campfire crackling so bright it made him look like he was glowing. No—he *was* glowing. The symbols on his followers' chests followed suit, and Ivy went cold with dread.

"He's not letting them into the void," she realized. "He's using their life force to open a door! He's *killing* them!"

Her voice rang through the forest just as vines wrapped around the vial.

The campfire glow faded. The symbols painted on the Circle's chests faded with it. Several of them stumbled, dazed with the weight of having their life force start to drain from them.

Christopher looked around wildly, the smile dropping off his face as his spell was interrupted.

"Who said that?" he yelled. "Where is she?"

"Shit," Ivy whispered. She hunched lower, curling her hands into fists. The vine tightened around the vial, but it was too late. Her uncle looked down, his eyes going wide as he noticed the plant tugging at it.

Christopher swore and yanked the vial off the staff. The vine around it snapped, and Ivy felt her connection fade.

One of the Circle members screamed and pointed at the cage Ivy was crouching behind. "There! Oh gods, the betrayer is there! She has the Skullstalkers!"

"The *betrayer*?" Ivy echoed weakly. "Come on, guys."

But it was too late. The Circle was preparing for battle, daggers flashing and bows emerging even as they steadied themselves. They didn't believe her, Ivy realized with a sinking heart. They still followed her uncle.

"Vale," Ivy said shakily. "Can you stand?"

"*I* can stand," said Zax gleefully, his remaining eye flitting hungrily around the people, some of whom were ready to flee. "Time to hunt?"

Vale grunted. He pushed himself to his feet, swaying. He could barely stand, but he made the effort to shove Ivy behind him, his fierce green gaze fixed on her uncle.

"Time to hunt," Vale agreed.

Then he charged.

Eighteen

Vale had never been more exhausted in his long existence.

His bones ached. His vision blurred. Even his skin throbbed, every beat of his heart bringing a new wave of agony as the wilderness void rotted.

But even a dying Skullstalker was lethal.

A mortal attempted to swing a sword at him. Vale clawed his cheek open and threw him into a tree. The next mortals ran at him with a net threaded with malblossom. This was irritating, but Vale barely felt the burns as he clawed the net to pieces and slammed the mortals to the ground with one swipe of his huge hands.

Ahead of him, Christopher stuffed the vial into his robes pocket and raised his broken staff. "Circle of the Jeweled Fist! Back into formation, back to your glory—holy HELLS!"

That last shriek was well-earned. Zax had streaked past him, his one unburned eye blazing purple with delight as he chased down the latest unlucky mortal foolish enough to run from him. He relished the chase more than the actual mauling, which was regrettable. It meant there were more mortals for him to take down.

Another net flashed over Vale. He swiped at it, but a third net soon followed. Then another. Burning lines of malblossom trailed across his face and arms, tangling his limbs until he was forced to stop.

Christopher dropped his staff into an attack position. Fire glowed at the tip, ready to shoot at Vale.

A malblossom-tipped arrow struck Vale in the leg. He staggered, falling to one knee. The net dragged him to the ground, pinning him down.

Christopher let out a triumphant cry and leveled his staff at Vale's face. Vale struggled, but he was too weak. The fire spell swelled—only to veer off into Christopher's panicked followers as the staff jerked upward.

Vale raised his head against the malblossom nets. Christopher's staff was bound to his arm, tangled in ivy. Vines climbed his robes, twisting around his limbs while he writhed.

"Help me," he barked at the Circle. "Somebody get over here and *help* me!"

A sharp, clear voice rang out through the clearing. "Nobody goes near him."

Despite the pain burning in his leg and the exhaustion threatening to overwhelm him, Vale smiled.

Ivy stood with her teeth bared and her arm outstretched, all of her trembling. Sweat streamed down her face, and blood trickled from her nose. But whatever toll the void magic was taking on her, she did not let it distract her from her goal.

Ivy's fingers closed. The plants around Christopher tightened, and he cried out in pain.

"Somebody cut me free," Christopher yelled. "And get back in formation so I can let us into the damned void!"

"Don't," Ivy snapped. "He's fooling you, can't you see? If you let him cast that spell, it will kill you all!"

The forest went silent. Even Zax stopped mauling his latest victim so he could watch the proceedings, his chin dripping with gore.

"He's never cared about helping us," Ivy cried, her arm shaking with the effort of keeping Christopher restrained. "I'm his last living family, and he threw me away as soon as it benefited him!"

A murmur went up through the surviving members of the Circle. Some of them reached for the symbol they had painted on their chests, as if remembering the feeling of having their life start to drain from them.

Christopher's lip curled. "Don't spew your lies, Ivy! You were always easily manipulated. What have these monsters told you?"

"I *was* easily manipulated," Ivy yelled. "Manipulated by *you*! I tried so hard to make you happy, to prove I was *useful*! And you would have let me get eaten so you could take back your 'rightful place'! You know what, Uncle? I think the king was right about you! You *are* a backstabbing, power-hungry wretch!"

Christopher scowled. "Enough of this! My loyal Circle of the Jeweled Fist, *fulfill your promise*!"

His hand flexed around his trapped staff. The forest lit up as the symbols on the Circle members' chests started glowing once more, the campfire flaring so high they almost reached the tops of the trees.

"No!" Ivy cried. "Vale, help! Get up!"

Vale tried to stand. But none of the mortals lifted the malblossom net off him. Especially when they started bleeding from their nose and mouths, muffling their choked cries.

"Wipe them off," Ivy yelled, turning her attention back to the mortals. "Damn it, wipe the symbols off!"

One freckled mortal's hand worked feverishly at her chest. She broke the symbol, and it instantly stopped glowing. She fell to her knees, gasping, before pushing herself back up and wiping desperately at the symbol of the man next to her.

"No," Christopher spat, gaunt and glowing in the campfire light. "No, don't! We must get into the void!"

But the freckled mortal's work was done: her husband's symbol was broken. He staggered into her, his eyes full of shock as he stemmed the blood pouring from his nose. He grabbed his wife's hand and tugged her away, stumbling into the trees.

"That's it," Ivy called. "Free each other! Free each other or die for him!"

Christopher let out an outraged cry as more mortals rubbed their symbols off. The only ones who did not free themselves from their symbols started to choke on their own blood, their eyes turning white and empty as the life left them.

"Zax," Ivy yelled. "Free Vale!"

But Vale was busy chasing the mortals who were foolish enough to run. The freckled woman screamed as her husband was dragged to the ground, his neck torn open by Zax's huge fangs.

The light from Christopher's spell faded. The impossibly high campfire died. The few mortals who did not save themselves fell to the ground.

"NO," Christopher bellowed as ivy trapped his now-useless staff against his chest. "It's not enough!"

"You—you killed them," someone yelled from the fringes of the group. "He *killed* them!"

"He did," Ivy said, her lips covered in blood trickling from her nose. Nowhere near as much as Christopher had done to his victims, but enough for Vale to know she was nearing her limit. "Just as he would've killed you all. Now, can somebody please *let* Vale up?"

No one moved. Not until Zax loped through the corpses, his chin still dripping with blood from chasing down the ones who ran. The man's freckled wife stood behind him, her face wet with tears and her husband's lifeblood.

"It is not good to burn," Zax said, inclining his scarred head at Vale. Then he began to cut the malblossom nets off Vale's trapped body.

An older mortal backed away, clutching a dagger at his belt. "What are you doing? It will devour us all!"

"He won't," Ivy said, muffled through the blood. "Not unless you attack him first."

"Or run," Zax added as he sliced Vale free. "If something runs from me, I will chase it."

He snapped the last rope. Vale stood, his knees wobbling underneath him. His vision blurred, the wilderness void a distant echo in his head.

He needed to get back. But he couldn't do that without the vial. He turned to Christopher once more, stalking toward him.

Christopher pointed his staff threateningly at him. At least, he tried. The ivy was still creeping over his limbs, forcing his staff to point up at the trees.

"You think this monster deserves the void?" Christopher spat. "You think *he* will make use of its resources? Only *I* can do that! *I* will take back our rightful place in this kingdom!"

Ivy curled her hand into a fist. The plants around Christopher tightened, and he let out a hoarse scream.

Vale strode up to him, every muscle threatening to give way. He was visibly worn and covered in burns. But Christopher's face still flickered with the appropriate amount of fear as he watched Vale approach.

"Come back to us, my beloved niece," Christopher called across the dead campfire as smoke rose into the trees. "I see your power now. You are glorious, just like you always wanted!"

"I never wanted that," Ivy said. "I only wanted a place that loved me. Something you could never provide."

The plants around Christopher's neck tightened. His eyes

bulged and turned bloodshot, his face flushing dangerously red as he choked.

"You..." Christopher fixed his red-spotted eyes on Ivy. "Y-you can't kill me. You don't have it in you."

Ivy's jaw tensed, but her hand loosened.

"No," she said softly as her uncle wheezed. "I don't."

Vale watched her expectantly. His body was withering along with his void. But he stayed on his feet, his claws ready. He had a promise to keep.

Sure enough, Ivy looked up at him, his once-timid offering turned otherworldly and fierce.

"But *he* can."

Nineteen

Ivy's uncle died in the middle of a scream.

Ivy watched his body fall to the forest floor and waited to feel something. Sorrow, or even regret. But all she could muster was weariness as she let her magic go, her plants stilling over her uncle's body.

"It is done," Vale announced, flexing the hand he had used to snap her uncle's neck. "Let us..."

He trailed off. He swayed, falling to his knees yet again.

Ivy stumbled toward him, wiping the blood off her face. The void magic had taken much from her, but she could still walk. She fell to Vale's side, ignoring the horrified stares from the people she used to call her own.

"Vale," Ivy said. "We can go now! Look, I'll get the antidote."

She reached through the vines clustered over her uncle's

robes and pulled the vial out of his pocket, holding it in front of Vale's drooping eyes.

"Look," she repeated. "I have it! Everything will be okay. We just need to get..."

She looked around wildly. The crack they had used to emerge into this realm had vanished, and the tree was simply a tree again. But they still had the circle where he had emerged so many times before. Even if the circle of blood above the stone slab was lost to time, there had to be remnants.

"To the door you carried me through that very first time," Ivy finished. "Okay? Just keep walking toward that."

She tugged on his arm. Vale grunted, then reached back to yank the malblossom-tipped arrow from his leg. His hand smoked as he clutched it. But it still took him a moment to gather the strength to throw it down.

Dread washed over Ivy in an overwhelming wave. This was no battle injury; this was the wilderness void dying and dragging its Skullstalker guardian down with it.

"Vale," Ivy whispered. "Are you going to walk to the door with me, or do I have to conjure some vines to drag you?"

Vale growled a strained laugh. Then he stood, legs quivering under him, fangs gritted.

Ivy put an arm around as much of his waist as she could manage. She could not catch him if he fell. But she could let him know she was here.

"Zax," she called. "Don't eat anyone else."

Zax's head shot up. He was sitting on his haunches, about to pounce on a man who was walking away a little too fast.

"But they trapped me," Zax complained.

Ivy winced. They had broken his horn and might have blinded him in one eye, not to mention the burns all over his body. But she also knew what *she* would have done a month ago. And she would not have helped him.

"I know," Ivy said, pushing Vale forward as he staggered toward the stone slab. "Leave them be."

Zax chirped mournfully. "Okay. But if they run, I *will* chase."

"Nobody run from him," Ivy called to the others. "His instincts take over. Everybody just... walk away slowly."

A woman made a hurt noise. At first, Ivy thought it was somebody who had been injured. Then the noise turned into a yell, and Ivy twisted to see Fawn Archton—the quiet, freckled wife whose husband had been torn to shreds when he tried to run from Zax—swinging a sword at Zax's head.

Zax caught her arm easily. And still Fawn fought, her cheeks wet with tears and blood as she struggled against him.

Zax looked at Ivy expectantly. "Can I take this one as a wife?"

"No," Vale croaked.

"Aw," Zax repeated. He released Fawn, who had to be restrained by several members of the Circle before she could be persuaded to drop the sword.

Ivy wanted to tell her she was sorry. Fawn was a new addition to the Circle and had been almost kind to Ivy at times. Ivy had the feeling that her life before the Circle was tough. From what Ivy had seen, her husband only made it tougher. But other than the Circle, he was all she had.

Vale staggered. Ivy braced herself, but Vale did not fall again. He leaned against a tree, his pale blue skin streaming with sweat.

"Almost there," Ivy urged. "Come on. Right there, can you see it?"

Vale growled weakly. He sagged, almost falling to his knees.

Ivy tugged on his antlers. She could hear people murmuring behind her, but she paid them no attention. They could do what they wished. She had a void to save.

After a slow, halting walk where both of them almost fell numerous times, Vale collapsed into the remnants of the circle he had been summoned into weeks ago. The stone slab sat in front of them, but Ivy ignored it. She had bigger things to do than reminisce over meeting the love of her life when he was dying in front of her.

"Good," Ivy cried. "That's great! Almost there. Now we just need to get back home. Can you do that, my love?"

Vale sucked in a breath. It was thin and ragged, his eyes glowing dimmer with each passing second.

Ivy choked back tears and fumbled for the antidote vial. She uncorked it with shaking fingers and poured a tiny trickle into the dirt, hoping with all her heart she didn't just doom the void by wasting a drop.

"Just concentrate," she told him as she shoved the cork back in. "Focus on your void. You have to get back, right? You have to take care of it. There's so much you haven't shown me yet!"

She shook him. Vale didn't move, his fading eyes trained blearily on her.

Ivy's stomach sank. Vale was clearly using all his strength to keep himself awake. How was he meant to get them back to the void?

"Okay," Ivy whispered. "All on me, then."

She closed her teary eyes and laid her hands in the dirt. The void's magic was still in her, even if it was weak. She focused, straining desperately for the magic she had felt when she was communing with the plants that tangled around her uncle.

Just find a crack in the void, she reminded herself. *Find it and yank.*

The dullest flicker lit up in the back of her head. Joy, so small she could hardly sense it. The void was happy to welcome them back.

Ivy grabbed it and pulled.

The faraway murmur of the Circle vanished. A sickly crackling replaced it, and Ivy opened her eyes to a horrible sight.

The sky was white and shattered. The bone-bushes lay limp, and trees crumbled. They were lying in the remnants of the silver pool, which was so dry that the dirt cracked under their weight.

Ivy climbed out of the hole and pulled desperately on Vale's antlers. "Hey! We're back, come on!"

Vale did not move. He was lying with the lower half of his body in the hole, the rest of him resting in the dirt. His green eyes fixed on her, the fires so faint that a spike of fear shot through Ivy's heart.

"It's okay," she managed. She pulled the vial out again, scrabbling at the cork with shaking hands. "I'm going to fix this, okay? I'm going to pour this in, and everything's going to be fine. You just watch."

She turned the vial into the hole. It trickled into the dirt, pooling around Vale's clawed feet.

Ivy watched desperately. The liquid did not glow, or turn green, or anything that she had been hoping for. It just lay there on top of the dirt, not sinking in.

"Nothing's happening," Ivy whispered. "Vale? Why is nothing happening?"

Vale did not answer. In the distance, trees crumbled and bushes died, and nightbeasts roared weakly.

Ivy wiped her cheeks. She had to do something. Maybe the void had been wrong, and this wasn't the antidote after all. But that didn't mean she could give up. She could find another way. She could channel her magic.

Ivy reached for her new magic. Nothing responded. Her hands were just her hands, and her mind was just her mind, nothing spectacular about them at all.

"Ivy," Vale rasped.

Ivy cried out with relief and cupped Vale's face in her hands. "Vale! We need to do something. Tell me what to do and I'll do it."

Vale's head drooped. At first, Ivy thought he was simply

exhausted. Then he spoke, and she realized that he was leaning into her touch.

"I was given... this void," Vale said, each breath an effort. "Always thought... it was the best gift I could ever be given."

"Vale," Ivy whispered. "Please don't."

"I was wrong," Vale murmured. "It was you."

With that, his green eyes went dark.

Ivy stared at him in disbelief. This had to be a mistake. She shook him hard.

"Vale," she cried. "Vale! Don't leave!"

Vale's unseeing eyes stared at nothing, dark and empty. Behind them, a tree crumbled into dust. Then another. The void was dead, and Ivy was standing in its corpse.

Ivy wailed. First in despair. Then, in anger, larger than anything she had ever felt.

"This isn't how it ends," she yelled. "I can— I can bring him back! I have magic, too. He said I could stay; he said I was going to be his queen. *You can't take him from me!*"

Her voice radiated through the void, strange and echoey. For a moment, all was silent, like a breath being held.

Ivy didn't notice. She leaned down and kissed Vale with all the desperation inside her. Her lip split open on his fangs, and still she kissed him. She kissed him until her sobs made it impossible, and she leaned back, hollow.

"Please," she begged.

Nothing replied. Ivy closed her eyes and rested her head on Vale's chest, ready to give up.

Then something impossible happened:

Red light bloomed on Vale's chest.

Ivy sat up, tearing her eyes open.

There was a red light rising out of Vale's chest. Folds of red swarming around each other, slowly forming...

"A rose," Ivy whispered.

The rose lifted into the air, circling slowly. Waiting, Ivy realized.

She reached out and touched it with one shaky fingertip.

The rose exploded, swirling into the sky and scattering over the trees. The sky bled comforting black, the crumbling tree trunks coming together again. Corpsefrogs began to croak, and bone-bushes sprang up once more.

The silver pool filled slowly underneath Vale. But still, he did not wake.

Ivy touched his cheek, shaky with disbelief.

"Vale," she said, her voice going strange and echoey once more as the void joined in, making her voice echo into the sky. "Time to wake up now, my love."

The faintest flicker of green awakened in the depths of Vale's eye sockets.

Ivy sagged with relief and threw her arms around him. After a moment, Vale returned the hug. Weakly at first, then so fiercely the breath was crushed from her.

Vale surged from the silver pool and pulled Ivy away long enough to stare at the void as it repaired itself.

"Ivy," he said. "You did it."

"*We* did it," Ivy corrected him.

Vale's green eyes flared. He gripped her chin and kissed her, licking blood from her lips. They stood there for a long while, trees cracking back into place and distant animals baying with delight as the wilderness void came alive once more.

Finally, Vale pulled back, leaning his cool, bone forehead against her warm skin. "I will find more assistants. You will have a good life here."

Ivy looked up. The dark sky twinkled expectantly, forming small circles of light that Ivy had seen back in the throne-room painting. What had Ivy felt the void say, back at the castle? *The caretaker must be fulfilled...*

"Actually," Ivy started as the first light-mote glided down. "About those assistants..."

Twenty Years Later

Vale's work was done for the day.

He retreated to their nest, his gait slow and relaxed as he approached the gauzy shelter that Ivy had constructed over it so long ago. Ivy claimed it was called a "tent," formed for the purpose of privacy. They could not have the assistants seeing them in the throes of pleasure, after all.

A strand of ivy pulled the thin tent door aside for him. At first, Ivy worried about her namesake plant populating his void. But it did not act as it did in the mortal realm. This ivy did not strangle or constrain. It simply existed, lining the void with beauty.

"Thank you," Vale told the plant that pulled the tent door open. He gave its leaves a brief stroke. The plant sent him a throb of joy, and Vale smiled and sent one straight back.

His queen's voice echoed from the depths of the tent, "Vale! I need your hands!"

"I am coming," he replied. He gave the vine another fond stroke, then headed inside the tent.

Ivy sat on the far end, perched in front of a mirror and humming while gathering her dark red hair with both hands.

"There you are," she said. "Do you mind?"

She held up her hair, which had grown more with each year she spent in the void. Nowadays it fell to her ankles. Braiding it was no longer something she could do by herself and required more than one single braid wrapped around her head to get her hair out of the way.

Vale took her hair and sorted it into sections, retracting his claws as he went through the familiar motions. Despite its length, her hair never tangled. Never caught or teared, no matter how many bone thickets she trudged into or teeth lilies she weeded. The wilderness void cared for its queen almost as thoroughly as its king.

Vale twisted her hair together in slow, practiced motions. When he started braiding her hair, he had done it quickly, as he had done all things. It had taken him years to halt the habit. Some things were meant to be savored.

"Harrier left this morning," Ivy told him.

Vale frowned. "That was this morning? Why did he not say goodbye?"

"He did! You were concentrating on drying the nightbeast hide. We decided it was best to leave you to it." Ivy smiled at him in the mirror, her rosy cheeks radiant as ever. "He will be back in the spring. But we should find a new assistant while he's gone. He mentioned he had someone in town who might be interested, but it depended on how that woman's mother was faring."

Vale growled absentmindedly as he wound her hair together. "I could always demand an offering," he joked.

"One offering was enough," Ivy said, her eyes glinting merrily.

Something chirped behind them. Vale looked in the mirror and saw a light-mote drifting toward them, glowing brighter than usual.

The light-motes had returned by the dozen as soon as the void had been healed. According to Ivy, who heard the wilderness void clearer than Vale ever did, they were fed by his joy. Once that vanished, so did they.

It was a confounding realization. Vale had always thought that he had grown tired of the work after the light-motes died. That was when his workload increased, after all. But the truth was, he had tired of the work long before he was left on his own.

Vale insisted it was because he needed variety. Ivy insisted it was because he longed for someone to share himself with. Privately, Vale believed her theory much more than his own.

And yet, his life was much more different with Ivy at his side. He no longer spent all his time in his void, and he spoke to many more beings than he used to, even before the light-motes left.

"Cxt'va," Vale said as the light-mote drifted closer. "What news?"

Cxt'va trilled.

Vale sighed. "Again? I will handle this. After I finish this braid."

"He will not," Ivy told the light-mote. She turned, taking care not to pull her hair from Vale's grip. "Cxt'va, thank you for coming to us. But I'm sure Geraldine can help you lift that log out of the way."

Cxt'va trilled again, rotating worriedly.

"She is *absolutely* strong enough," Ivy declared. "Have you *seen* her arms since she returned? She had been cutting wood all winter! She could lift Vale if she wanted!"

Cxt'va spun an anxious circle. Then it made a decisive hum and flitted out of the tent, off to find one of their several mortal assistants.

Ivy turned back and met Vale's glowing eyes in their reflection. "Was it always that anxious?"

"Always," Vale said, not unkindly. He had not remembered how fond he was of his annoying brood of light-motes until they rushed back into his life.

He tied the braid off. Ivy's long crimson hair hung in a thick braid to her waist. She made to stand up, but Vale stopped her.

"Not yet," he told her.

He took the last handful he'd left loose and braided it quickly. Then he tied it around her head, pinning it into place with a bone-pin the void had gifted her two decades ago: one of its many wedding gifts.

Ivy laughed, touching her makeshift crown. She rarely wore

her hair like this since it grew too long for all of it to fit on her head.

"What is this for?" she asked. "Is it a special occasion?"

"Does it need to be a special occasion to give my queen her crown?" Vale replied. He kissed her hair, pushing one last strand of crimson hair into place as he grew his claws back out.

Ivy's gaze caught on his claws. Her eyes were hungry, and Vale's tail flicked in anticipation.

Ivy stepped toward the nest in the center of the tent. But she did not climb into it yet.

"How are the rib-thickets?" she asked.

"They are content."

Ivy nodded, running her fingers over the fur lining the nest. "And the root-deer?"

"The herd is thriving," Vale said. He walked behind her, catching her in his arms. "The void is well. There is nothing that must be done."

Ivy shifted happily in his grip. When Vale ran a hand down her braid, she leaned into his touch. But she did not turn in his arms.

"We need to find another assistant," she pointed out.

"We also need to see the new crop of shadow trees in my brother's void," Vale said. "It is not urgent. Why do you tease me so?"

"Because it's fun," Ivy said sweetly.

She turned in his arms, finally. Vale placed a claw under her soft chin and let the love into his expression. She had not delayed him because she found it *fun*, as she claimed. At least, not entirely. She had done it because she wanted to feel desired.

Vale stroked her cheeks, pressing his claws gently against her plush skin. "My strange gift. How glad I am that you were given to me."

"Thank you for keeping me," she replied, as she always did.

Vale kissed her deeply. His fangs nicked her lip, and Ivy murmured her appreciation as he sucked on the small spark of pain.

"We have time before we must leave to find another assistant," Vale said, rubbing his thumb over her bloodied lip. "We could find a heatbloom."

On cue, a heatbloom plant rose out of the dirt between them. A rose bloomed with it, ivy twining up the rose's stalk and then curling around her finger.

Ivy laughed, curling her finger to greet the plant. Then she looked up at Vale expectantly.

"Weren't you the one," she began. "Who said there is always more work to do?"

"There is," Vale said. "But it is being taken care of."

"Not *all* of it." Ivy tugged at the makeshift crown around her head, as if thinking of the responsibilities it held. "If I get lust-pollened, I'll be useless for days."

"You do not need to be useful," Vale reminded her. "You only need to be you."

Ivy's eyes went shiny. She kissed him again, and Vale licked the blood left on her lip.

"In that case," Ivy said as she pulled back. She raised her

head toward the tent ceiling, her eyes flashing void-green. "Don't let anyone in the tent unless the sky is crumbling!"

The tent rippled in a nonexistent breeze, confirming its response.

"Thank you," said Ivy sweetly.

She ran her hand over the heatbloom between them. Then she dug her finger into the center.

Golden pollen poured out from the petals, filling the tent. Ivy giggled as it coated her skin and covered the braid that Vale had so carefully tied into her hair.

Vale waited intently. Sure enough, Ivy's breath began to pick up, her pupils swelling. The scent of her desire consumed the tent as readily as the pollen, making Vale growl and dig his claws into her hips.

Ivy gasped, her eyelids fluttering as his claws drew the slightest amount of blood. She grabbed his antlers, frenzied in a way they had not experienced since the last time they had done this. They tried to limit their pollen doses to twice a year. But sometimes they got impatient.

Vale threw her into their nest and climbed on top of her, chuckling as Ivy tore at his robes.

"Off," Ivy gasped. "Take them *off*!"

"Anything for my queen," Vale said.

He shed his robes. Then he dragged a claw down her dress, which changed depending on her mood. Today's was a short, breezy pink, and it parted under Vale's claw like any other.

Ivy made a desperate noise and grabbed for him.

Vale held her down, enjoying how she squirmed against his touch.

He had been numb to his own desire for so long. Then this mortal had come into his life, and he could ignore it no longer, no matter how much he tried to resist. He was not an emotionless beast built to perform tasks. He was an animal with animal needs: hunger, sleep, lust, and a love so deep he could barely contain it.

"Not yet," Vale said. "Are you not forgetting something?"

Ivy frowned. Then her mouth dropped open, twisting to watch two strong ropes of ivy knot around her wrists and bind them into the nest.

"Oh," Ivy gasped.

"There is more," Vale assured her.

Ivy looked down and groaned as she saw the large, bulbous vine that was sliding up her thigh. It was not wet, but that did not matter. Ivy was slick enough for all of them. And if she was not, the magic would make it fit painlessly.

Hence why Vale dug his claws into her hips, drawing the smallest amount of blood.

Ivy moaned, bucking up against him as the plants held her down. "Vale! *Gods*, I need it."

"You will have us both," Vale assured her. "Which hole would you like us to fill, my queen?"

Ivy grinned up at him, her cheeks dark red. "Both."

"As you wish," Vale growled.

The vine entered her ass. Ivy's mouth opened on an ecstatic cry. But still her legs opened wider, waiting.

Vale pushed inside her other hole. The stretch was exquisite, even with the magic easing the way. He rocked deeper, feeling the vine do the same in her lower hole.

Ivy moaned. A petal brushed Vale's antler, and he looked up.

Roses were growing from the tent ceiling. He laughed and thrust deeper still.

Ivy whimpered. "I love you so much."

"Always," Vale assured her.

He leaned down and kissed her. Then he leaned back to watch the petals rain down on his wife's gorgeous, pollen-dusted body, and mated her until the entire void was awash with blooms.

Special Thanks

Thank you so much for reading Given, the third book in the Skullstalker Brides series!

If you want to support me, please leave a review on Goodreads, Amazon and any social media of your choice.

Acknowledgments

A big THANK YOU for the Kickstarter backers who brought this book to life! I couldn't have done it without you.

Now let's hear it for the publishing team! Edward Giordano, formatter extraordinaire, and my fabulous editor Naomi Darling, my cover artist Rana Dela (ranadela_x on Instagram).

Lastly, thank you to sarahinwanderland on Threads, who does not know me but is the reason that Vale has foreskin.

About the Author

Isabelle Taylor writes sweet, steamy fantasy romance. She works in a bookstore in New Zealand and has a Creative Writing Masters from the International Institute of Modern Letters.

She can be found on Instagram and TikTok @isabelletaylorauthor.

instagram.com/isabelletaylorauthor
tiktok.com/@isabelletaylorauthor